Acclaim for S D1055819

Of Drag Kings and the Wheel of Fate

"This disparate duo's lush rush of a romance—which incorporates reincarnation, a grounded transman and his peppy daughter, and the dark moods of a troubled witch—pays wonderful homage to Leslie Feinberg's classic gender-bending novel, *Stone Butch Blues*."
– *Q Syndicate*

"*Of Drag Kings and the Wheel of Fate* is a novel about family, not the family we are born into, but the family we choose as adults. It is a book about the courage to be who you are, about the choices we make, and the honesty to follow through on those choices. Smith has invented a story that is full of love, with intense characters who along the way discover parts of themselves for the first time ... A novel that makes a difference. It is filled with understanding and respect for the varied forms that love takes. It discards standard definitions of family, love and gender. Smith's story reminds us that people cannot be put into neat little boxes. Life is fluid and changing, and as Smith so succinctly conveys to us, we must be too." – *JustAboutWrite*

Burning Dreams

A story of "...intentional family, healing of hurt loved ones, celebration of genderqueers, and just enough mysticism to intrigue even skeptics..."
– *Books to Watch Out For*

"Smith's style is unique. It envelops the reader with memorable and inspiring passages that are the meat of the story. In my opinion, she is one of the best writers of prose in lesbian fiction today. There is so much emotion mixed with wisdom and clarity in *Burning Dreams*. It is a story about discovering who we are even in the face of adversity, and it is about creating families to support us so we are not invisible. It is intense yet subtle too, like a velvet hammer. The author again challenges our preconceived notions of love, gender, and what is acceptable. Simply put, she makes us think." – *JustAboutWrite*

By the Author

Of Drag Kings and the Wheel of Fate

Burning Dreams

Put Away Wet

Beth —
All things come
through love —

PUT AWAY WET

— Smith

by

Susan Smith

2008

PUT AWAY WET
© 2008 BY SUSAN SMITH. ALL RIGHTS RESERVED.

ISBN 10: 1-60282-025-2
ISBN 13: 978-1-60282-025-8

THIS TRADE PAPERBACK ORIGINAL IS PUBLISHED BY
BOLD STROKES BOOKS, INC.
NEW YORK, USA

FIRST EDITION: AUGUST 2008

CREDITS
EDITORS: CINDY CRESAP AND STACIA SEAMAN
PRODUCTION DESIGN: STACIA SEAMAN
COVER DESIGN BY SHERI (GRAPHICARTIST2020@HOTMAIL.COM)

Acknowledgments

Madeline Davis, writer, activist, librarian—I owe a debt of gratitude for instilling in me, when I was a puppy, a sense of pride in the history of the Buffalo lesbian community, for her decades of activism and writing, and for taking me by the scruff of the neck and telling me to go be a librarian.

Dedication

To Celia White, Poet, Librarian, Goddess—a kindred spirit, an inspirational crafter of words, and always my friend. Everyone should be lucky enough to have companions of wit, passion, and creativity. I'm lucky enough to know their Queen.

CHAPTER ONE

I know that ass, Jocelyn "Joey" Fellows thought idly, while tearing through the skin of the peach she'd purloined from the kitchen just as her shift ended. Her teeth punctured to the heart, red flesh whiskering around the stone, juice like summer climaxing on her tongue. The chef had ordered the peaches for a dessert. They were too tempting to ignore. Joey spent her shift trying to resist the scent, then gave in with a sigh and grabbed one on the way out the door. It left her in the odd position of biting into the peach, juice making its sticky trail down her wrist, when the ass in question rose like a glorious Beltane moon, framed in the window of the late-model bronze sedan parked in front of Joey's apartment. She'd thought little of it, passing by on her way home from work. Tourists often took advantage of Days Park's proximity to the bars of Allen Street and parked there for the evening's revel. All it meant was another Tuesday night drunk stumbling into the bushes, until the advent of that particular ass, popping up like a buoy on the tide.

It took Joey two full strides past the sedan to register the thought, then respond to it. It couldn't possibly be? The familiarity question became critical. There weren't that many people she'd ever been on speaking terms with their anatomy at that level of intimacy. One, to be brutally honest. It had been months since she'd seen her ex-girlfriend. Now, while strolling home from work on a Tuesday night, Joey spotted what looked remarkably like her ex-girlfriend's ass, in the tangled act of love in the backseat of a car, parked in front of her apartment. God couldn't hate her this much, Joey thought.

Joey ghosted onto her porch, creeping, shrinking back in the shadow of the round pillar. The bronze sedan was parked directly in front of her house. A quick glance around the U-shaped park showed plenty of other empty spots. True, the house was just three in from the top of the U, and thus desirable as a parking spot for a bar crawl. But it was Tuesday! Who in their right mind got so besotted on a Tuesday night that they mated in a car?

Well, it was summer, Joey admitted, and granted that might have something to do with it. Buffalo's winters were long and brutal, and the first appearance of a sunny day made everyone a little crazy. People ran through the streets all summer like children.

It was possible that what she was, increasingly, witnessing was an act of spontaneous passion and not at all an attempt on the part of her psychotic ex to literally rub her face in it.

I have to get a grip on this, Joey thought, then shook her head. *Not grip. Have to get rational about this.* The first thing to determine, she was sure, was the identity of the ass in question. That would open new avenues for inquiry, or settle the matter. This necessitated close observation. Scientific observation, needful and just. Not at all voyeurism, Joey assured herself.

The first determination that Joey made, from her partial view around the column, was that the couple in the backseat were at the start of their amorous adventure, or nearly so, as they were struggling to remove their clothing. The first flesh sighting had been courtesy of what appeared to be a difficult pair of jeans.

The second determination was that they were both female: a brunette with close-cropped hair, facing the porch, and the blonde with the spectacular ass, veiled and preserved by her Godiva hair, with her back to Joey.

That left the identity question painfully unfulfilled. Joey's ex had long blond hair and a spectacular ass. The question would she actually plan such a thing was still open. A giveaway tattoo, a birthmark, an interesting scar might have helped, but the back before her was smooth and tanned, and pressed up against the door.

That was one of the annoying problems with getting dumped, Joey thought. You see your ex everywhere, in every face, every turned profile, every billboard and grilled cheese sandwich. She might just be suffering under that failed romance delusion.

Visual identification got increasingly difficult when the pair tumbled back onto the seat, obscuring them from view. They had, Joey soon realized, cracked the window. The night was still, clear, perfect to convey the softest sound a mere ten feet. Now Joey had to use her imagination and fill in the actions to the varied moans and moist sounds drifting her way. Her ex had always had a theatricality about her sexual performance that intimidated the hell out of Joey, in the beginning, in large part because of her inverse experience level. She'd never had a girlfriend before. Thus, she had no comparison. When her instinct told her that her ex was exaggerating, or even inventing her response out of whole cloth, she couldn't really ever be sure.

This sounded mighty convincing. Enviable, really. Joey closed her eyes. It had been six months since she'd had sex. That was an impressive moan. Blood started to burn in Joey's veins. What was the brunette up to? And on a public street? Why couldn't she have been invited?

But she'd been there, those moments when the bed, any bed, was too far away and it had to be now. The first tangled, sweaty weeks of a new love.

Through the clear summer night Joey could hear the stranger coming, each wave preceded by anticipatory barks calling God, God, God; met at the gate of the lips with a moan high enough to be a squeak, a sound of pain or endurance, and followed by the fluttering down of feather-like breaths.

That wasn't her ex. With that determination, she was left lurking in the shadow of a pillar, listening to a stranger's carnal dance. Abashed, aroused, Joey eased the door to the apartment open, trying not to jangle the keys. The sound of the blond woman coming haunted her until dawn, preventing rest or release.

❖

Joey was having a spectacularly bad day. Wednesday nights at the Heritage Room were rough under normal circumstances: overbooked with privileged suburban assholes all enraged that they might have to wait an extra fifteen minutes for a table. It didn't help that the hostess on Wednesdays was a bit of an airhead, only employed because she had great tits and was screwing the night manager, and often she had access to coke.

Joey's tables were double-booked, leaving her in the weeds for hours. The busboy had called in "sick," meaning the Sabres were playing and he was sitting in his underwear down on the West Side with a twelve-pack yelling at the TV. Thanks to a sauce event, she'd had to change her sparkling white dress shirt, mandated by management to be as pure as a child's innocence and bright as the hope of salvation (or at least as bright as the hope of a Super Bowl ever being won by the Bills).

She was a bit of a stickler for her uniform. There had to be standards, is all, so she took it home and guarded it like a soldier. She never washed the black pants with other colors, only cold water, to keep the trueness of the black from running into a mediocre and indifferent charcoal. She mended and washed and starched and ironed until it was the firm, brilliant, and unequivocal mark of a professional. Joey was a waiter and had pride in it.

The Alfredo Incident, as she thought of it, had destroyed the crispness and purity, the meticulous beauty of her shirt. The replacement she kept in her locker was a good oxford cloth button-down. Not a bad shirt, all things considered, but Joey had to suppress a shudder of discontent when slipping into the less-than-white cloth and adjusting the less-than-firm collar. Cream. Off-white. Unstarched. It set the tone for the rest of the night—just a bit off. Passable to look at, but inside, Joey knew she wasn't looking her best, and it took the spring out of her step. Not having slept the night before didn't help, either. It left her feeling adrift, unanchored, haunted. She started seeing her ex's face in heads of lettuce and folded napkins.

She managed an understanding smile for the woman who'd doused her in Alfredo, comped the meal out of her own pocket, and charmed her way around the rest of the four top until a reasonable tip could be expected. All while not grinding her teeth at the money she'd lost due to the customer's flailing. *Honestly, who gestures with a plate full of Alfredo? Every one of these tourists should work for a night in a busy restaurant. That would bring back their basic humanity.*

No, that was unfair, Joey reminded herself. No sense in letting anything ruin her night. Externals only. She had a job to do. Smile, charm, and run her ass off. The performance continued. There was a brief escalation of disaster when the chef 86'd the tuna without informing the wait staff. Joey had to patiently endure a profanity-laced tirade from the chef, part of the cost of crossing the border from the dining room into his kitchen, when she dropped the order off. The customer, who she'd read as intractable from first glance, turned out to be phlegmatic about it, and ordered the salmon. *Just goes to show, you can't always assume the worst,* Joey thought, happily speeding back to the kitchen to drop the salmon order. Maybe things were looking up.

"Sweetie, be a jolly good fellow and bring the desserts to table six."

Joey looked up, ready to stab her sommelier's tool in the arm of anyone calling her sweetie, but restrained the impulse when she saw the angelic face of her best friend and fellow waiter Steven "If you have to ask, you can't afford me" Price. His blond hair was artfully tousled, his scalpel-sharp cheekbones bounced light, his eyes glistened a golden summer's day blue. He was working the look. He knew the effect of his beauty on men, women, and children. He knew he could get away with murder, or, more likely, get away with a coy smile and a hint that he'd like someone murdered, only to find the body gift-wrapped on his porch later.

It didn't matter a whit that he and Joey were gay as geese. Beauty has its own convincing aura. *Pretty people make more money, get away with more, live privileged lives,* Joey thought. Steven was more than pretty, so he traded on it shamelessly. "I'll develop a personality when my looks fail. Humanity, compassion, all that rot you're mad for, Joey. I'll feed the homeless puppies and house the hungry," he was known to say.

"Steve, angel, cherub, incubus, no. Run your own damn desserts, I'm in the weeds."

The look of pleading became a trembling lip, the glassy-eyed hint of a tear being withheld, the wounded confusion of a child slapped away for being too affectionate. How did he do that? Not a hint of insincerity in it; it squeezed Joey's heart, even though she knew better. Growing up together in Eden, New York, he'd always been able to sucker her into taking the fall for him. She knew she was being played like a baby grand.

"But they are a fabulous group, bunch of locals out for some anniversary or the other. They expressed interest in the building, and who knows that crap better than you? You could slip them crème brûlée and a history lesson. Then, sugared up and indulged, they will tip generously in the warm glow of their appreciation. And I'll split the tip with you."

He hit her weak points. Tonight was going to be tight, with comping the dinner earlier. She might not make a lot of money, and rent was due. Joey also loved this district of the city passionately and had made a study of its history and architecture. Allentown had been the arts district for over a hundred years, awash in artists, writers, musicians, replete with theater and poverty and literary gypsies. It was the place to go to escape a conventional life, such as the conventional life in a farming town for a young girl, abandoned by Fate to being born into a small hearty Middle American town as a raving homosexual. It looked to Joey, at seventeen, like the ninth circle of hell. She had to get away. Steve wasn't about to let her go anywhere alone, so they ran off all the eighteen miles to Buffalo to go to college, and discovered Allentown. Someone wanted to hear her talk about wonderful, magical Allentown, her home? Could she resist?

"Tourists. You want me to entertain the tourists," Joey said, trying to sound bitter, but already sold.

Steve heard the acceptance in her tone and smiled triumphantly. "They're neighborhood. Over on Mariner."

"Well, that's different. I'll always help out the neighbors."

Steve blew her a kiss and was gone. Committed now, Joey grabbed the tray of desserts and headed for Steve's table. She took them in with a waiter's automatic glance, discreetly assessing the audience: number, age, position, appearance: four adults, two couples. One was man/woman, one woman/woman. The women were as different as night and day: One femme, pretty, blond hair to her shoulders, in her late thirties or early forties, with an expression of such humor and compassion that it was hard to picture her not smiling. The other was butch, handsome, black haired, tall, in her late twenties or early thirties. She was a pretty boi, but not genetically male. One butch read another. They were nicely dressed, but funky. Artists, queers, locals. Her people.

Joey's smile was genuinely warm. "Good evening. Steve asked me to bring your desserts. He mentioned that you had some questions about the building's history?"

The man smiled back at her, handsome, balding, bearded. Total dad. "That's right. We live just down the street, but we'd never been in here before."

"It's like that for a lot of people. How often do we get to Niagara Falls, with it in our backyard?" Joey said.

The butch was sizing her up, Joey could feel it. She smiled at the woman holding the butch's hand. They were a stunning couple, in close physical proximity. It could be the first flush of romance, but Joey had served too many celebratory dinners to mistake the air of a well-established couple. They were just in love, the bastards.

There was nothing more disgusting to the brokenhearted than a couple genuinely in love after years together. Maybe this was a part of Steve's intent, to make her see living evidence that a queer couple could be happy. *Go on, flaunt it, Steve. I'll get you back for this.* Joey wasn't in the mood for exhibitionary evidence. Love still made her queasy.

So she turned her attention to the man and woman. It didn't help much. They too looked happy, in a quiet, deeply satisfied way. The woman was regarding her with as much intent, dark humor in her opaque eyes. It made Joey shiver, being so clearly seen. She was used to serving and performing, and going unnoticed. This woman was watching her like a snake.

"Well, to give you a little background, this building was built in 1831 as a neoclassical structure, modeled on the Harvest House mansion in Rhinebeck, New York. Silas Riley, who made his fortune running transport along the canal, hired the firm of Leowen and Hark to design his home. The Riley family lived here for a decade before tragedy struck. Silas lost his fortune, and within the course of a year, his wife and three of his children. The rumor is the house was too haunted for Silas, either with grief or ghosts, so he closed the house up and eventually sold it. The Heritage Room has been in this location for forty years. Before that, this building was an insurance agency, and going back to the turn of the century, a hotel."

"And a brothel," the scary woman said, unblinking.

"That's right. Not too many people know that. Back when Allentown was still known as Lower Bohemia."

"It feels like a brothel."

"A wonderfully checkered past, like most of Allentown," the dad said.

"Like most of us, Joe," the butch said, grinning at him. Joey started at the name, but she was talking to the dad.

Time to go. Any more conversation would be intrusive, as they were already talking with one another. Her waiter's instinct for the poised, delicate moment to leave flashed red: now, grab the tray, go. Yet something held her, trapped like a dragonfly in amber, near the circle of their happiness. These four people had great love among them, and it was warming to stand nearby, even as an observer. For a moment, Joey let herself linger. Reflected happiness was, just maybe, not as nausea inducing as it was enviable.

"Can I get you anything else?" Joey asked, reflexively. They had everything they needed. The bastards.

"No, I think we're all set, thanks," the dad said.

"Great. You folks have a nice evening. I'll have Steve come by with your check. Happy anniversary," Joey added, to the queer couple.

The blond woman started, then smiled. "It's our ten-year. Are you psychic, too?"

"No, ma'am, just a waiter." It was the exit line. She bowed, formally, and spun on her heel.

The snake woman caught her hand. It was odd enough that Joey did not react, she was held by the woman's mesmeric stare. "You will be all right. Not for a while, but eventually."

Joey felt the room shift into some hazy ghost space, a purple twilight yawned through the fading walls. "Uh, thanks. Have to run."

She pulled away, nearly barreling into another patron who was just pushing her chair back. All she caught was an impression of black hair, the turn of a woman's profile. It shocked her back into reality, the artful dodge of her hips to avoid contact in the press. Then she was in the kitchen again, and safe.

"Weren't they fun?" Steve asked as he grabbed his next order.

"Yeah. Little weird, but fun. Thanks a boatload for waving the Happy Homosexuals in front of me. You know that people in love disgust me." Joey slammed her tray down on the counter.

"We can't hold it against them. Cheer up, maybe they are really bitter and alienated inside, like we are!"

"No. We're just going to die alone in the gutter."

"We'll die alone in the gutter together," Steve said, holding his hand over his heart.

"Oh shut up, Princess Optimism."

"Kiss my shiny golden ass, Mr. Crankypants."

The sparring kept her awake, sharp. It kept her going. Raised in a family of exceeding politeness and minimal warmth, Joey had trouble expressing emotion without sarcasm. It had to be filtered through humor, teasing, even bitterness. Nothing could ever be unalloyed. She could feel love, but that welling gratitude for her best friend was communicated the only way she knew how. He gave as good as he got, and so they sniped and snarled their way through the maze of intimacy. Far easier to say *I hate your bloody guts* when she meant *I cannot make it without you*. Their relationship was like a straight guy buddy movie without all the unconscious homoeroticism.

Another round on the floor, desserts, drinks, coffee, checks. An hour slipped by unnoticed. When she looked up, it was ten o'clock, the end of the seating. Joey allowed herself a cup of coffee in the kitchen, leaning against the wall. Time to rein the horses of her pulse in and start wading through the end-of-evening damage, before she could crawl home and mourn her poverty and ruined shirt. With any luck, she could replace it in another week or two.

The kitchen door swung open and the hostess came in, motioning to her. "Joey, you have a table."

Joey sighed and put the coffee down, half full. What

self-important narcissist wanted a table after the seating was done for the night? A judge, a lawyer, a sports figure? Maybe someone the owner knew. Steve crashed out of the kitchen, past her, spinning back into action for his last floor round. He was back almost instantly and hadn't even served what he was carrying. A fire? A rat running across the floor? She could smell the smoke of impending disaster before his face, contorted with concern, turned to her.

"Sweetie, I am so sorry. Let me take it."

She knew. It was like clamping her teeth on lightning, but she knew. Psycho Barbie had finally shown up. *No, please, dear Lord, no, not now. Anything but this. Take a limb. Pry out my eyes with a clawfoot hammer and throw kosher salt in the sockets.*

The blonde last night must have been a harbinger, an ass of doom, presaging the coming of the Dark One. In a way, Joey had spent every moment at work for the last six months looking over her shoulder, expecting and dreading this moment like a penitential on her knees awaiting the apocalypse. It was the end of days, her ex, confronting her at work.

CHAPTER TWO

W ho do these bitches think they are, coming into my place and demanding food after the seating is done?" Mario, the chef, was swearing up a storm. "They aren't getting any fish, no meat. The pasta is put away. Stupid low-rent motherfucking dog-sucking puta can lick my sweaty low hangers." He continued with his profane chant as he started working. A knife flashed against the sharpening steel to the rhythm of the words.

His tirades seemed to give him strength. Joey envied him his freedom as master of his domain, never having to face customers unless he so chose. Freedom to despise those he served as plebeians, beneath him. She didn't have that luxury. Her life's blood, her pay, depended on her ability to smother what she felt and produce a cheerful, acquiescent mask. "No, Steve. I got it. Clean up my own mess and all that jazz."

She squared her shoulders, smoothed her apron, and hit the floor. *Keep your thoughts locked behind your face. Behind the bone. Don't let them get to the skin.* Joey was aware that her body was moving through the now largely empty room with a clipped and professional stride. She watched, like a camera, like a ghost, as her body approached the table. She should be trembling, howling, clawing, rending in a fury of emotion. She felt nothing but a pleasant, hollow chill.

This must be one of the new girlfriends, then, perhaps number 3, or later. Girlfriend 3.0? More like Meal Ticket 3.0, year or two older than Joey, androgynous, well-dressed, expensive fabrics. Well done, she'd moved up the economic food chain. Likely a grad student. Probably law, she had that smug look. Joey kept her attention on 3.0.

"Good evening. Would you care to see our wine list?" Remarkably, she sounded calm. *I should win an Oscar for this performance, or stop in to the hospital to see if I'm dead yet. I have no pulse*, Joey thought.

"What do you think, baby?" 3.0 asked her date.

"Wine, yes. Hello, Jocelyn, how are you?" Psycho Barbie asked, smiling brightly at Joey, as if they had just happened to visit a restaurant, and just happened to sit at her table. As if they were old friends. Or even friends of any sort.

Nice fake sincerity, Joey thought. *You wouldn't last half an hour working a service job.*

She looked the same. It had been months, merciful months, since Joey had laid eyes on her. The skin was the same, tanned to a Thanksgiving glow. Joey wondered if her ass looked the same, perhaps pressed up against a car window. The hair, perhaps a shade brighter, more paint-by-numbers golden highlights. The same snub nose, the same cold blue eyes. Had anyone ever told her that her smile never reached them? Why hadn't Joey noticed that before?

Psycho Barbie had been the first great love of her life. An accidental meeting, while both were freshmen in college, led to jaw-dropping paralysis over this gorgeous creature. Joey had never seen a girl so beautiful, at least, not in person. She was a picture out of a catalog, someone who should always be posed with the ocean at her back and a servant, off camera, carrying all her supplies. She was beautiful, in a cultivated American heartland corn-fed Aryan blond and blue-eyed way. Practically a copy of the doll. She was also very used to other people doing all the heavy lifting for her. It was how she got the enduring nickname, from Steve. He was the one who later amended it to Psycho Barbie, when he got to know her character. "Pretty and plastic, but there is something wrong behind her eyes. Listen for rising background music while you are showering."

After six months of bliss, she and Joey had moved in together. Steve had warned her then that it was a bad idea, but Joey didn't listen. How could she? She was in love, for the first time. That made her legally insane and prone to fits of self-destruction. What was she to do? It was her sneaking suspicion, while still drunk on the newness of her first love, that Steve was just jealous. He didn't have his best friend to play with anymore. Besides, he and Psycho Barbie were inverted reflections of one another—too blond, too pretty, to get along. That turned out not to be true. Steve disliked her because Psycho Barbie treated his best friend like dirt.

Joey was easily intimidated by deeply attractive women, and took that feeling as a sign she wasn't good enough to speak with them. Beautiful women made her feel clumsy, awkward, like a farmhand. Whatever power and charm she might have possessed went right out the window. Joey had no sense of herself in the face of beauty. That this girl, this ridiculously pretty girl, paid attention to her made no sense. Joey was butch, average in her own estimation, inexperienced, unremarkable. But they'd met in a first-year women's studies class, and that lent a glamour to the working-class butchness that Joey lived. Psycho Barbie enjoyed wearing Joey's butchness as a badge of honor. Liked that she worked twenty hours a week as a waiter while attending school. That she didn't have a lot of money, but seemed happy, anyway. How Bohemian! How artistic! It helped that Joey was warm, and engaging, and social, knew and enjoyed a portion of the gay community, had friends and interests. That started to change as soon as they lived together.

It took a while for Joey to see it. Some of the signs she recognized along the way—Psycho Barbie's willingness to ask for increasingly difficult or expensive things that Joey was then obligated to provide, her dislike for all of Joey's friends, her desire to isolate and separate Joey from her social rounds. The small manipulations that became large ones. Psycho Barbie's coursework in psychology was always more important than Joey's studies. At least it was a real field of study, one that would lead to a job. What plans did Joey have for the future? How was she going to support them? After two months of living together, Psycho Barbie stopped working. Joey already had a job, she was the butch, she was supposed to support them. Didn't Joey want to support her? The only way to do so was for Joey to drop out of school. Psycho Barbie insisted, and Joey complied. Wasn't she butch? Didn't a butch provide for her girlfriend? Joey had never actually had a girlfriend, and was still figuring out what it meant to be butch. All she had to go on were stories, and Psycho Barbie's opinion.

Sometimes, sometimes it seemed so sweet and perfect, like when they would dress up, she in a suit, her girl in a dress, and go out on the town. For that night, or that evening, Joey would hold doors and pull out chairs, practice being gallant and feel, for the first time, handsome. It is one thing to long for a woman, to feel broken and torn up when she leaves, to need the sound of her voice to the point of pain. It is another to have her in your lap, to know you can move your hand to the back of her neck.

It was glorious. It never lasted.

Three years into her degree, she dropped out to be a full-time waiter and a full-time supporter of her partner. This was it, her future. This relationship was all she had, all she was. Two months later, Psycho Barbie broke up with her and told her to move out of the apartment leased in Joey's name.

In the end, after three years, Joey had nothing but a broken heart, a mountain of bills, and her best friend. Steve took her in to his falling-apart, run-down apartment in Days Park, in the heart of Allentown. Joey couldn't afford anything else. She was still paying the rent at her old place and would be, until the lease was up. Psycho Barbie had been Joey's first great love, and her first lover.

Joey was left in ruins. Nothing, nothing was left she recognized of herself. She'd failed on every level. Where, she wanted to cry out in agony, were her role models? How was she supposed to deal with this? Who was she supposed to be? Steve held her as she sobbed and threw her guts up, for weeks. Called in sick for her at work. He kept her drunk, every night after work, for a month. Fed her, slowly, moving from toast back to more solid food. Loved her, in the simplest, most pervasive way. Kept her alive.

It took Joey two months to feel like she could breathe again. After four months of having her best friend at her side every day, she started to recover some of her self. She smiled. She played. She would hang out after work, go the bars with him. Make rotten, self-serving jokes about unnamed former girlfriends. But she would not allow the mention of ever dating again, and refused to talk about maybe, someday, going back to school. Her life, as she saw it, was irreparably broken. Now there was endurance, her last, and only, virtue. No more love, ever again. At twenty-two, her life was already finished. She was just too damn stubborn to fall sideways into the grave.

Joey was set to move out on a Saturday and was home

packing on Wednesday when Psycho Barbie started dating again. She didn't have the simple human decency to wait three days to cuckold Joey. She stepped across her body in the living room to march out to her date. Likely, she'd been doing it all along. Joey knew of two indecent relationships Psycho Barbie had had while they were together, and was sure that there were more. When Psycho Barbie set rules, they were only for other people. She was beyond human restraints and considerations, like fidelity, loyalty, or friendship. She'd been through at least two girlfriends since, by report. And now she was here.

"Fine, thanks. Here's the wine list. Would you care to start out with any appetizers?"

"Give us a minute to decide. Bring a bottle of the Red Penguin '92, but if you don't have it, don't bring the '93. Bad year for grapes, too dry. I'll consider a '95, but only if you bring the bottle price down."

Great, 3.0 was an ill-informed wine snob. The worst kind, aggressively ignorant. Joey had read the same article last month in *Wine & Food for Boneheads*, speculating that the 1992 Red Penguin was the best vintage from that winery in decades and advocating that people buy only that year. In fact, it tasted like cats had been using the grapes as litter. The article was written by a cousin of the vineyard owner, and was a ploy to unload back stock. In any other case, Joey would have offered a test glass of the '95, or even better, an Australian import for a comparable price with a much better body and finish. But the customer was always right.

"I'll check on that '92." She could see them bend their heads together, whispering about her as soon as she walked away. Joey nearly tore a neck muscle resisting the urge to turn back around. *Calm. Stay dead calm. This will all be over eventually.*

Joey brought the Red Penguin 1992, as requested, and with cynical theatricality, white towel over her arm, showed the label to 3.0 before uncorking with an elegant turn of her sommelier's tool. She then poured a glass and handed it deferentially to 3.0, waiting to see what would happen. The woman swirled the wine so aggressively it spilled drops onto the tablecloth. *Good, an inadvertent libation to the food gods*, Joey thought. *Go ahead, taste it.* 3.0 did, and smacked her lips.

"That will be fine."

Joey bowed and poured a glass for Psycho Barbie. No taste in either of them, anywhere.

Appetizers were chosen, dithered over, then re-chosen. Wine flowed. Dinners came. Throughout it all, Psycho Barbie put on a great show of having the time of her life, laughing loudly at 3.0's every word when Joey approached the table, setting her hand on 3.0's arm. *I get it*, Joey thought, *you've never been happier and you have to have me notice.*

Every time Joey went back in the kitchen, Steve was waiting, ready as a corner man taking care of his boxer. He handed her coffee, he rubbed her shoulders and set the next plate in her hand for delivery. When she was sent back to the kitchen for more bread, he had it already cut and in the basket, the tea tray prepared, everything on the side. There was no need for words between them.

Joey briefly considered taking kitchen justice on them, but her stubborn work ethic prevented the fantasy from getting too satisfying. *Pretentious, fussy assholes*, Joey thought.

Steve handed her a plate. "It'll be over soon, sweetie. And then we can get stupendously drunk."

"Monumentally." For a moment, Joey's chin trembled. "Promise?"

"I've got your back, sweetie. Always. Come on now, you've been doing so great. Don't let her see you cry."

"What kind of person does this? This obscene charade?"

"Wait, let me consult The Book." Steve spread his hands, as if he were holding an immense, invisible tome. It was Steve's conviction that people often appealed to books for authority on any topic, so he started doing the same. His book could be read only by him, but he was willing to share the harsh but beautiful knowledge therein. He pointed to the imaginary page and read. "A totally insecure, sociopathic asshole. A waste of carbon. Usually an ex."

Joey took a deep breath and went back on the floor. Now her table was the last in the restaurant. The kitchen staff was nearly done with the cleanup, the dishwashers were already mopping. But Psycho Barbie and 3.0 lingered like a foul odor.

"Jocelyn, I hate to mention it, but the fish was a little overdone," Psycho Barbie oozed.

The fish had been perfect. As evidenced by Psycho Barbie's plate, it had been good enough to devour down to the bones.

"I'm sorry to hear that. Shall I take it back?" Joey asked, looking down at the nearly empty plate in great concern.

"No, it's not worth it. I was able to eat it anyway. But I thought the chef should know, the food is usually so good here."

"I'll be sure to tell him." Just after the next Ice Age. "Would you care for anything else? Coffee, desserts, perhaps another bottle of the '92?" Joey asked, obsequious.

"No, we're done. You can bring the check." 3.0 said.

Joey left, gladly, and went to print the check. She made no pretense of including Psycho Barbie in the list of potential providers for the meal. Clearly, 3.0 had been selected for her ability to open her wallet. She went through the dance with 3.0, taking her card and retreating to the station to run it. Usually the hostess would, but now she was blowing the assistant manager, so she could be blowing otherwise by and by.

While at the station, Joey fought her way through the computer, cursing the slowness. She felt the hair stand up on the back of her neck, then a hand on her arm.

"Joey."

She froze. There was no way to react, now that the formal positions that allowed them to interact were gone, transgressed. Now she wasn't a waiter, giving a parody of perfect service. Now she was just a very tired, very stressed-out twenty-two-year-old girl forced to wait on her ex, her first love, and her current replacement. Joey had never been there before and had reached the end of her imagination. She hadn't rehearsed.

"It's so good to see you. How are you, really?" Psycho Barbie asked, looking at Joey's lips.

"I'm fine."

"Still living with Steve in that hole?"

"Still with my best friend. And yeah, it's what I can afford, with the rent on our, I mean, your place."

"Well, you signed the lease; you are responsible for it. You don't believe in keeping your responsibilities?"

"You know that I do," Joey said quickly, nettled.

"Or maybe you only mean what you say when you feel a certain way. If how you feel changes, you don't have to keep your word."

"I keep my word," Joey said sullenly.

"Only when you feel like it. That's not loyal; it's purely situational. It allows you to get away with being so selfish."

"Stop it! You're twisting everything I say. You know I'm loyal. I keep my promises. I'm still paying the rent, and we broke up months ago."

"You have a legal obligation to pay the rent. It doesn't mean anything about how you feel about me. You once made promises to me, too. I don't have any idea how you feel about them now that they're all broken."

"Stop it. How can you even say that? You were my whole life. You left me."

Tears were coursing down Joey's cheeks and she couldn't stop them. Psycho Barbie got her guts in a basket weave and kept her from thinking clearly. Psycho Barbie played on words that, for her, were meaningless, bright, glittery toys to toss into conversation.

"This isn't about blame, Joey. I think we both changed in the relationship. If there is going to be blame, there is plenty to go around."

There was nothing Joey could say to that. They had both changed in the relationship, her into a doormat and Psycho Barbie into a controlling narcissist. Joey tried desperately to reassert the forms of public association. She was a waiter, Psycho Barbie was a customer.

"Your check is ready."

Psycho Barbie laughed, a simulacrum of a delighted chuckle, and clapped her hands. "Now, Joey, don't be like that. You feel over your head in an argument, you close up like a turtle. It's comical. I didn't come over here to argue. I came over to genuinely see how you were doing. It's been a long time since we talked. I miss you."

"Yeah?" Joey asked, hating the very pathetic timbre of her voice, but not being able to stop. Approval from this person had been her world for years, approval dearly bought and paid for. Yet still she responded like a whipped dog.

"Of course, silly. You know that." Psycho Barbie played with the collar of Joey's shirt.

"I don't know anything."

"Well, I do."

It was wrong, it was against all evidence of her senses, her memory, and against every word Steve had spoken to her for the last six months, but Joey felt it. The stab of pleasure, threaded through with pain. The taint of hope. Her veins opened like an addict's. Psycho Barbie leaned in and just brushed her lips against Joey's.

"Plus, there's something I needed to talk to you about."

Joey's head snapped back like a trout on a hook.

"The last phone bill came. You have some charges that carried over."

Joey knew that the frozen expression on her face was horrid. Knew that the blood was draining away from her heart; false blood, as the organ was already necrotizing. Nothing she could do about it.

"How?" Joey meant, How could this be?

Psycho Barbie heard it differently. "Just shy of a hundred."

Joey's hand went immediately to her pocket. "But that's all I've made tonight."

"Well, the bill is overdue. I know it's in my name, and so it won't be important to you now that your feelings have changed, but it is important to me. My good name is important to me. Even if you don't care."

Joey handed her the folded bills without counting them. "It's all I have."

Psycho Barbie took the money with the neat clawing motion of a professional. "That will be fine. I'm glad we got this chance to talk, Joey. And that you did the right thing. You look good. All that hard work agrees with you."

Psycho Barbie then kissed her on the cheek and took the

credit card slip back to the table and 3.0. They looked over the bill, looked back at Joey, then signed it. 3.0 got her coat, took Psycho Barbie's arm, and they were gone.

Numb, Joey wandered over to the empty table. She picked up the slip.

Tears made the numbers blur, but she blinked them away. Could that be right? It was the final straw, the capstone on an evening of horror. 3.0 had left her a five percent tip.

CHAPTER THREE

Down Allen Street they went, arm in arm, gloriously drunk, nerves swimming in dopamine, finally, no pain, just a floating sensation and a happiness with a slight hysterical edge that the smallest touch might tip into sobbing or rage. She and Steve swayed like sailors just off the boat, singing one of his musical rewrites with an obscene gusto, this evening a selection from *Oklahoma!* to the tune of "The Farmer and the Cowman."

> Oh, bulldyke and the faggot should be friends
> One queer likes to push a penis
> The other likes to chase a Sal
> But that's no reason why they can't be friends
> All queer folks should stick together
> All queer folks should all be pals
> Bulldykes dance with farmer's daughters
> Faggots dance with their Brokeback gals!

Past the row of bars and cafés and small quirky shops their path wended, past and into Nietzsche's and the Old Pink, past Mariner and College Streets, to the end of Allen Street, where it elbows into Wadsworth. Days Park abutted the curve. There, on the second floor of a house, Steve kept a three-bedroom apartment. It was cheap, it was convenient, it suited him. His bedroom was the largest and faced the street. Outside, it was a hovel, but inside, Steve had worked wonders. It was a slightly cleaner, better-decorated hovel. Joey had the back bedroom, the one where you had to step down, under the doorway where she had gone mad killing spiders. She had left their legs still clinging to the ceiling surrounding the smear that was their bodies, smashed with the end of a long, narrow cardboard box. The third bedroom had belonged in sequence to a series of Japanese exchange students: Kenichi, then his friend Nobu, then Ken's girlfriend Kaori. Ken had gone back to Japan, but felt comfortable leaving his spirited Kao-chan with the gay man and the dyke. Oddly enough, they provided both safety and a warm environment.

Steve had a rich older lover in Puerto Rico whom he saw every few months and who would call the apartment and ask for Steve in his beautifully modulated, softly accented voice. Steve had also had a local lover, and others. Joey was used to making coffee for anyone who showed up in the kitchen in the morning in any state of undress, without asking them who they were. It surprised some of the boys when she would hand them a cup, say good morning, and walk away without questioning them or pressing for explanations.

There was a cat that lived with them, Joshua. He was a big gray tiger tom with a head like a rock and a rat's tail, incongruously, on his football player's body. Josh used to live at Cybele's, the café down the street, when Steve had been a waiter there. While some customers were charmed by a cat in the window, some others were less charmed by a cat on their plate. Josh moved in with them, and he still had his quirks. He liked to come in the back door off the balcony, into Joey's room. The only problem was, he'd jump up from the fence to the balcony and scream his head off until she got out of bed and let him in. Kao-chan called him Josh-u, or Bakka-neko—stupid cat. He was a charming bastard in his way, but she was on to something about his essential nature.

Joey attempted the very shallow step onto the front porch and promptly fell flat on her face.

"That's gonna sting in the morning. You okay?" Steve asked, swaying above her.

"Can't feel a thing. S'fuggen loverly."

"Wonderful. I have another bottle upstairs."

"Tequila?"

"Five percent."

"Tequila."

They checked for Kaori, calling out loudly and crashing off the walls as they pushed one another up the stairs. She wasn't home. They sat, or collapsed, on the couch in the living room, the bottle and two shot glasses before them. Steve poured for both of them.

"Women suck," Joey said, holding the shot.

"Not my kind of toast, but why not. Women suck!" Steve cried out with great enthusiasm, throwing back the shot. "Men suck, too, sweetie. If you're lucky."

"Love sucks," Joey said, pouring again.

Steve took the bottle. "You know what your problem is? You are fixated. You must not be getting sucked enough."

"Oh, go on."

"I'm serey-o, serious. The best cure for a broken heart is a good, er, suck."

Joey looked away into the distance, terrible and stern. "My heart is an impenetrable fortress. I shall never love again."

Steve started giggling and fell off the couch. From the

floor, he cast himself on Joey's feet and flung his arm across his forehead. "O bottomless pit of sullen depression! No one is more wretched than I. I shall never love again."

Joey kicked him off. "Fuck off."

Steve stood up and brushed himself off. "That's what I'm talking about, sweetie, not love. You need a good romp in the hay. Bit of the beast with two backs. Saturday night special. No love involved."

"I'm a lesbian. Lesbians don't do that," Joey said, miserable. Though there had been that couple in the car. But no, not for her. There was no way out of the tunnel she was in. The light was failing, the stars were veiled, jackals were abroad in the necropolis. Gibbering spirits drooled and howled in the reeds of a stinking swamp. Joey looked out across this landscape, and despaired. Steve interrupted this particular train of thought with a reasonable question.

"What do lesbians do?"

"Far as I can tell, go on one date, then torture each other for years."

"You need an online personal ad," Steve said brightly.

Joey looked at him, incredulous. "Oh bloody right."

"Serious. It's what I do for a broken heart. Jump on gayboy4play, and half an hour later, I've forgotten whatever his name was. How else do lesbians find one another in this electronic era?"

"Freshman women's studies class?"

"Come on. It'll be fun! We can make up your profile together. I'll get my laptop. You have another shot. It'll be a game!"

"Okay. But just for sex. I don't want to date anybody."

Steve came back with his computer, a present from an admirer, and started typing. "I'll ask you the questions and fill it out. What do you want your name to be?"

"Joey?"

"Can't let them know who you are. The Internet is full of scary people."

"What's your name?"

"Goldengod69."

"Of course it is. How about Ima Waiter?"

"Lady in Waiting?" Steve suggested.

"I'm not a lady." Joey picked up the bottle and poured herself a clumsy shot.

"Butch in an apron?"

"Lives_to_serve."

"That's not bad. I'll make it all Internetty. Lvs_2_Srv. Perfect."

There was entirely too much typing for Joey's taste, so she ignored Steve and downed the shot. Much better. She considered the bottle, then considered her glass. Something was missing, some step or process in the alchemy. She kept applying the light in a bottle, the golden tears, to her wounds, but the wounds didn't heal. Perhaps she felt them less, for a time, but she was still bleeding on the carpet.

"I don't think I'm doing this right," she said to Steve, cradling the shot glass in her hand. He glanced, then went back to typing.

"You pour, then you drink."

"Not that, this." Joey's expansive gesture took in the room, the neighborhood, the city in a single arc.

"You're not doing what right?"

"Everything. There's nothing..." She stared at the glass for a moment. "How? They tell us what not to do. Everybody does. I'm real clear on what not to do." Her head was too heavy; she slumped back on the couch. "It's like I'm not supposed to exist."

"No more shots for you."

"I'm serious. When I was a little kid, you know, plenty of people told me what to do. Do this, and it is good, and right, and true. This is what little girls do."

Steve patted her knee. "They were wrong more than they were right. Plus, you weren't a model little girl. At least since fifth grade. Before that, I can't speak from experience."

"I know, and it got harder every year, you know? You can get away with some stuff at seven, eight, ten. Being a tomboy is cute and all. Feisty. If you're still a tomboy at fourteen, you better be an athlete. I'm not. I just hung out with guys because they made sense. Well, you made sense. Girls don't make any sense. But if you're still a tomboy at sixteen, eighteen, the words change."

"Changed long before that for me, sweetie. I was past what was allowed by the time I was five."

"Yeah. So here we are. Now we know what we shouldn't be. It's all we hear anymore. You shouldn't look like that, or talk like that, or date like that, or act like that. Don't belong in church. Don't get uppity about getting married. That is not for you. I get it. I don't belong. But the funny thing is, I'm waiting to hear the next words, you know? I'm with you, I understand everything I can't be, or do. So, after all that, what's left? What can I be? Who am I supposed to be?"

"You can be happy."

"I don't think so. Not anymore. I think that part of me died."

Steve took the glass away from her and stretched her out on the couch.

"It's just sleeping, sweetie. Just sleeping. The good stuff doesn't die."

"How do you be happy?"

"You learn to say yes. Life offers you tasty things, you say yes. A pretty boy asks you to dance, you say yes. Girl, in your case. Say yes. The more yesses you have stored up, the easier it is to learn to say no. You're not starving anymore."

"Not starving anymore. Yes."

"You're getting it."

"I'm gonna close my eyes for a bit. Read me the questions."

"Butch or femme?"

"Me? I'm not that drunk."

"Yes, you are. Not you, who you want to meet. You like the strong, handsome type, maybe in for a little bromance with a fellow butch? Or do you faint for the fair femmes of the family?"

"Oh. How am I supposed to answer? Everybody's cute."

"Okay, we'll go with everybody's cute. How about age range?"

"Legal is nice."

"Fine, 18–60. You're easygoing. What about men?"

"No men."

"Couples?"

"No men."

"Got it. I'll just fill in the rest, make it sing. We need a picture." Steve looked up to find Joey passed out on the couch. He sighed and went to get his camera.

"Would-be ethical slut?" Kaori asked.

"Excuse me?" Joey asked, shocked. She almost dropped the frittata.

Steve glanced up. "Your personal ad. I finished it up, gave it some pizzazz."

"Please tell me you are kidding."

"Uh, nope. I was bored after you fell asleep, so I finished it."

Joey pushed him out of the way and grabbed the computer. There it was, complete with a picture of her, taken after she'd passed out on the couch. The tagline read: *Would-be ethical slut lacks experience, please train me.*

"Great screaming mother of God."

"The picture is quite nice," Kaori said.

"One of my better," Steve agreed.

In the picture, Joey was sprawled carelessly on the couch, reclining odalisque in her waiter's black pants and white shirt. Steve had opened a few buttons to give a deceptive glimpse inside, artful shadow or actual flesh? Her arm was thrown across her eyes and her face turned, three-quarters, obscuring her identity. It was a lovely image of female masculine abandon.

"I will kill you. I will salt your hide and hang it on a fence to dry. You are not publishing that. Dear God, Steve, we were drunk! I was just talking!"

Steve got very still; his eyes got very round. "I thought you were serious."

"I am now. Delete the bloody thing before anyone else sees it."

"I posted it last night. You've had six hundred and twelve page views already."

She felt a tirade build, with words like *death* and *blood* and *thunder*, with flashes of disembowelment and castration and fire ants. It nearly shook her teeth loose from her jaw, the effort not to vomit it forth. Joey took a deep breath.

"Plus, there are the e-mails," Steve added sheepishly.

"How many?"

"Hundred and fifty," Kaori said, gleefully.

The numbers were enough to give her pause. Joey was balanced between her annoyance at Steve and her intrigue. What harm would come from reading a few? She could always kill Steve later. "Okay. More coffee. We're going to read them. Then I will decide how, and if, I'm going to kill you."

"Read the good ones to us," Steve said.

Joey scanned the first few. Bill and Joan wanting the obvious. Partygirl2007, whose boyfriend liked watching her.

Hitting Delete, she said, "I didn't realize lesbians were rarer than vampires,"

"Rarer than Viagra, which I see you're being offered, again," Steve said. "Something you're not telling me?"

Where were the lesbians? It came to Joey, sadly, with a low, clinging chill: sex only. Not wanting a relationship was the kiss of dyke death. The ad didn't even read *seeking friends or bridge partners*. Just sex. It had been the tequila, and Psycho Barbie, and the dish of ashes where her heart should be. Joey didn't think she was capable of love anymore. Not really. Joey continued hacking through the forest of phallus. There had to be a lesbian in here somewhere, hiding, maybe in a cave, under a bush.

"Men just love lesbians," Kaori said, staring at the screen.

"I'm butch, for hell's sake! That's like shaking hands with your brother. It's too much like being a gay man. Men don't want butch lesbians."

Steve looked her over. "You look like you slept on a couch, but I'd do you."

"Thanks, and please never say that again. You know what I mean. Straight guys go for the pornalicious fake lesbians. The whole porno dyke world is a femme sleepover, where we braid each other's hair and get manicures until the right penis comes along and jumps in the middle." Joey shook her head.

"Not interested in middles?"

"I'm not a middle of the roader."

"What if a middle of the roader writes to you, seduced by that hot picture?" Steve buffed his nails against his chest, admiring his own artistry.

"Awesome. She can't bring her boyfriend/husband along, not even to watch. But if she's free, well, hey there, sailor."

"Helloo, nurse!" Kaori said.

"Exactly."

"Oh my God. Seriously, I think I found an actual lesbian!" Steve hooted.

Three heads bent to the screen.

"How can you tell?" Kaori asked.

"No mention of penis deployment, husband, or boyfriend. Plus, she says she's a lesbian."

"Read to me, Steve."

"From: SinisterFemme. 'I can train you, my handsome girl. Meet me for coffee, and we can discuss the possibilities. I'm 41, poly femme dyke with a streak of the outrageous, a primary partner, and a sense of play. Your ad says sex only— well, can't promise that. Sex is one form of communication; we will likely have others. There will be passion, and laughs, and lots and lots of affection. I can promise that I won't ask for a relationship, other than friendship. I won't take up all your time, or invade your life. I can also promise I will treat you with respect, no matter how ephemeral or lasting our connection. You'll leave me with a kinky smile on your face. I won't be the love of your life, but if you and I click, I can be the love of your night.'"

Joey's mouth hung open. "Wow."

"You think she's for real?" Kaori asked.

"Only one way to find out. Write back and say yes to coffee," Steve said.

"What if she's a serial killer? Or a guy? An axe-murdering serial killer guy who lies on the Internet to lure inexperienced young dykes to their death?" Joey asked.

"Relax, I do this all the time. Set the meeting for a public place, let friends know where you are and when to expect you back. Kaori and I will come along, just as backup. If we think there's any bad vibe, we'll pull you out." Steve patted her shoulder.

"A minute ago you were fine, now you are scared?" Kaori asked.

"A minute ago it wasn't real. Okay, granted, you seem to have been right, Steve. The online thing works. If I'm going to do this, I should do it all the way. This is an adventure, right? To have adventures, you have to say yes to anything that comes along, let your path find you. So, I'm saying yes. Let's have coffee with SinisterFemme, and maybe I'll keep on saying yes."

Chapter Four

This was ridiculous. Here she was, sitting in a coffee shop on Elmwood, waiting for SinisterFemme, who had said in her laconic reply that she would be wearing a red carnation.

Joey had to wonder if that was some sort of joke, or code. Red carnations were the Ohio state flower, chosen to honor President William McKinley. McKinley was famous primarily for being shot to death in Buffalo. The coffee shop was half a mile from the site. Maybe SinisterFemme knew her Buffalo history, too? That would be interesting. Red carnations probably meant a hundred other things, maybe she was just really flower literate? Fliterate. Maybe SinisterFemme would be disappointed that Joey couldn't interpret the flower the right way and would storm out in a fury.

Joey could just go home, kill Steve as she'd planned to in the first place, and have done with it. Perhaps sensing her thought, he waved from his post by the muffins. Kaori, the other half of the backup team, was not far from him, reading the newspaper in a casually obvious way. Their presence brought Joey back to her second thoughts, that she was about to make a grand and public fool of herself. Lesbians were rarer than vampires riding unicorns. What made her think that this one even existed? She was probably a man. Or Chris Hansen with a camera crew. This was ridiculous, and she should get up right now and walk out of this coffee shop, past what looked like an actual woman walking toward her table. The time for dithering was over. It was particularly hard to dodge humiliation. Potential romantic humiliation. She was no good at dodging that, given her track record. If it were possible to always make the wrong choice, romantically, then that was her oeuvre.

The approaching woman couldn't be a lesbian. Suburban, forties, a little plump in a wonderful "I have hips and love them way," long, curly brown hair, full makeup including red lipstick at four in the afternoon. Painted nails in a pomegranate shade. Smartly dressed, slightly daring, skirt and sweater set. Heels. Low heels, sure, but heels. Lots of bracelets that sang when she moved her arms, clustered around her wrists, rings, earrings, necklaces. Motion, lots of motion, everything moving in all directions, round and swelling and cascading. This was a suburban woman, pretty, ate organic vegetables, did yoga and maybe jogged a bit, studied belly dancing for fun. Belonged to book clubs. An attractive woman, but one that Joey wouldn't have given a second glance to in any other context. Straight attractive, pleasant, the polar opposite of a dyke. And ten thousand miles away from kinky, or sinister.

Joey felt very young, and very queer, and very much out of place. Yet there, pinned as a corsage on the swelling glory of her carefully restrained right breast, was a red carnation. McKinley's death certificate. This must be SinisterFemme. Joey wasn't wearing a flower, but she saw the woman glance at her, smile with plump lips, and know her. A quick glance around the rest of the room seemed deliberate, with a fraction of a second's lingering on Steve, who was staring. Then she pulled out a chair and sat at the table.

"You must be Jocelyn."

"Joey. Yeah. I mean, yes, I am."

"Naomi Zimmerman. You know, like Bob Dylan."

Joey looked at her blankly.

Naomi sighed. "You are young, aren't you?"

"I guess so."

Everything about her was round. The curve of her eyebrows over the most perfect and liquid heart-stopping black eyes Joey had ever seen, the round bow of her lips, the round motion of her hands, roundness of hips and legs and arms. Round round get around. To be embraced would be to be enveloped. Enthusiastically. Joey felt more than a little lost. What was she supposed to say? Naomi was looking her over with what felt like evaluation, a weighing and measuring as sharp as her waiter's eye. What visual scale was she registering? It was unpleasant being on the other end, knowing that Naomi was judging her.

"So, Joey. What do you do? Are you a student?" Naomi asked.

"I'm a waiter."

Round eyebrows got rounder. "I see. So Loves to Serve was restaurant related."

"Lives to Serve, but yeah."

"So you're not a sub."

"Uh, I guess not. I mean, I don't know." This woman had experience. Maybe even Experience. Why would she waste a glance at a practically inert twentysomething?

The whole thing was coming out in a hot rush, and there was nothing she could do to stop.

"Look, I'm sorry. I'm twenty-two, I've had one girlfriend ever, and she stomped my heart like a herd of buffaloes. I got really drunk the other night after she came to the restaurant and I swore I would never love again. Steve suggested an online ad, and he did the typing. I did shots and I woke up on the couch the next morning with a bunch of e-mails. I want to be cool, I want to charm you, but I don't know anything."

"How long were you with her?"

There was warmth and genuine sympathy in the question. Joey could feel it. So she unfroze, a bit, and relaxed into the entire Psycho Barbie story. The whole sordid, gut-wrenching tale of woe. It took fifteen minutes to get through, to relate the miserable tale of her first and only love.

Naomi whistled, impressed. "You were rode hard and put away wet. You sure you still want to be gay?"

Joey shrugged. "I am gay, want to be or not."

"What do you want, Joey?"

"I want to know what I'm doing. I want to have some experience. I want a woman's body on top of me, under me, and I want to know what I'm doing while I'm there. I want to be slick, and together, and confident. Sex would be awesome. But I can't date. I just can't. I don't think I will ever love anybody again."

"Deep breath. Okay, I have a sense of where you are coming from. You should have a sense of where I'm coming from, before we start coming."

Joey smiled a little.

"Good, you do have a sense of humor. I was worried. I can train you, Joey. I can give you what you are seeking. But you'd have to be willing to listen to what I say, and to do what I ask, within negotiated boundaries. You have to be willing to push yourself. I can be very strict." All the lovely warmth went out of Naomi's tone.

Joey sat up under the suddenly stern black eyes. It was like being in front of a drill sergeant. A very compact, round drill sergeant. Yet this was experience, being offered to her.

She would have to learn to say yes, build up the experience bank, before she learned to say no. Willing to push herself? That was the reason she was here.

"Yes," she said.

"Yes what?"

"Yes ma'am?"

"Yes, Mistress."

"Yes, Mistress."

"Good, Joey. Aren't you a handsome boi. Straighten your shoulders."

Joey did so, with alacrity. There was something so self-assured about Naomi that it made Joey jump to respond. Naomi seemed to know exactly what she wanted, and wasn't willing to have anything else. It was thrilling. Just using her proper title put everything into a new light. Joey liked the way Naomi was looking at her now, frankly, thoroughly. Under that gaze, Joey felt more interesting, more attractive than she had in months.

"I do love a handsome boi. I don't often find one to play with. You have lovely hands. I wonder what your fingers feel like."

Joey looked down at her hands, resting on the table top. To her, they looked rough, burned and cut in the restaurant way, hands that worked for a living. But Naomi looked at them and licked her lips.

"Have you ever wanted to be someone else?"

"Mistress?"

"For a time, to escape, to become someone else. Live under someone else's skin. Be a hero, or a rogue, or an adventurer?"

"Sure, Mistress. Who hasn't?"

"You can, with me. You can be many people."

Joey smiled, felt the rise of excitement. This wasn't like anything she'd ever done. Joey had always had a weakness for older women, from the perennial crushes on grade school teachers to the elaborate yearning of the teenager for the high school instructor. She liked women who smiled warmly at her but held the reserved power of approval. Naomi promised to be all that, and more. A teacher she would be allowed to have a crush on, at least.

"You have access to a computer at home?"

"Yes, Mistress. My roommate has one."

"Wonderful. We're going to play a little game, during the week. I'll send you the start of a story, and you finish it for me. Can you do that for me?"

"Yes. I mean, I think so, sure. Mistress."

"Good, Joey. Let yourself go, and have fun with it."

Naomi wrote a few things down. "Here's my contact information and my address. Be there, Friday night at eight p.m. You don't work Friday nights, do you?"

"Saturday and Sunday. I swap some Friday nights."

"We'll negotiate in the future. This Friday, eight p.m. Pack an overnight bag. And only ring the upstairs bell. Do you have a car?"

"No."

"No?"

"No, Mistress? I take the bus."

"That's fine. I'm on the 20 line."

"Mistress?"

Naomi was repacking her purse. "Yes, Joey?"

"Can I ask a question? Is the flower a McKinley joke?" It felt foolish, but she had to know. It would tell her something essential about Naomi, if she communicated with the world in a series of arcane, inside jokes, constantly talking with her city, like Joey did.

Naomi looked surprised. "It is. How did you get that?"

"It was the first thing that occurred to me."

"You are a curious boi, Joey. I like that. I'll be in touch."

The first e-mail came at six p.m., subject: *The stables.*
Joey had commandeered Steve's laptop, and locked herself in
her room and read.

> It is a stormy afternoon, dark and
> somber, with lightning flashing in the
> sky. I have just burst into the stables,
> furious. My matched palfreys were
> supposed to be hitched to my surrey for
> my afternoon ride, and here I find them
> in their stalls, idly munching alfalfa.
> The stableboi, handsome and sullen, is
> leaning on hir pitchfork. I look over at
> the brute, insistent that my anger have
> a place to rest. I am the Lady of this
> household, my wishes are law. My riding
> crop slaps against the crisp tan of my
> jodhpurs. My high leather boots gleam
> in the fading light. "Explain to me why
> my horses are not ready," I demand.

That was it. Joey read it, again and again. This was the
start of the game, and it was her turn. Clearly, she was the
stableboi, Naomi was the impatient Lady. What scene was
she trying to build? She was angry and wanted a release of
emotion. Well, two ways to go with that, really. Apologize and
let her rant, which might be the behavior she expected from a
servant. Or challenge her, and give her something to push back
against. That appealed to Joey. She was forever apologizing

in real life, it would be fun not to. The stableboi herself had already been cast as sullen. Why not make that arrogant as well? So Joey wrote:

> I was leaning on my pitchfork, resting for a moment from the backbreaking labor of mucking out the stalls, when Her Ladyship came bursting into the stables demanding to know why her horses weren't in harness. Anger gave her high coloring, added a snap to her flashing black eyes, and the slap of her riding crop suggested she wanted to use it on me. Rich people hate to be inconvenienced, even for a moment, on one of their whims, or so it seemed to me, from my post in serving them. They also didn't have much sense. "Lady," said I, leaning still on the pitchfork, "if you use the eyes God gave you, you'd see it is pouring down rain and lightning. Nobody is going riding today."

Over to you, Mistress, she thought. Anticipation hit as soon as the Send button was hit. Now she had to wait. Joey checked her e-mail again a few hours later, and was profoundly disappointed to have no reply. How long was she expected to wait? Had she said something wrong? That curl of anticipation and fear stayed in her stomach all night. She checked her e-mail again at dawn and found Naomi's reply.

> "I don't pay you to lecture me on the weather," I say, my anger rising with the stableboi's shocking boldness. No one spoke to me in this fashion! "I

planned on having a ride today. It is your duty to provide me with one. If the weather is not cooperating, you will have to use your imagination." I threw this last comment to the stableboi with an impatient flip of my hair, back over my shoulders. I was furious! The stableboi would have to work to bring my anger down. I seized the pitchfork she leaned on away from her, and cast it down at her feet.

That was direct. Naomi wanted riding? She'd get riding. Joey felt the blood heat along her veins, felt the thrill of power assumed.

The Lady threw my pitchfork down. Angered, I seized her shoulders in my hands, made strong from years of working with horses. Her eyes widened when she felt the strength of them, fingers like steel, scoring her shoulders. I shook her soundly. "You'll get your riding, you spoiled rich brat." I flung her down in an empty stall, into a bed of fresh hay. "The riding you so desperately need." Her shirt opened like a flower, buttons torn away, breasts blossoming into my work-roughened hands. The riding crop flailed, weakly, at my back, more urging me on than stopping me. "You wanted to know what my hands felt like. Feel for yourself."

Send. She would have to wait until after work to check for response.

Hours later, twitching with impatience, Joey opened her e-mail and felt the hot sparks dance on her skin. Naomi had written back.

Straw pokes at my back, tangles in my hair. My crisp jodhpurs are unbuttoned and thrust down to my ankles, billowing around my boots, until they are impatiently pulled off and tossed away. Those magnificent rough hands, those hardened fingers splay my wet thighs like a prayer book. The stableboi, true to her word, gives me the ride I demanded, fucking me with her iron fingers. "More," I gasp, head thrown back, my boots locking together behind the stableboi's back. The riding crop, haphazardly, finds the backs of her legs. Lightning explodes above us, rain slashes at the roof. I have always loved the feel of powerful thews between my thighs, the galloping rush of blood and freedom, the rising together into a perfect whole, woman and beast. Yes, the joys of riding. I have had a wonderful time down at the stables, perhaps I'll have to come again, on a rainy afternoon.

Joey leaned back on her bed, breathing deeply. Wow. So this was what playing with Naomi would be like. Friday better come soon.

❖

Joey looked down at what she was wearing and had an attack of fear. *Jeans and a vendor T-shirt with dancing cheese on it? Oh, that's slick, handsome.* It was a hot night, hot enough not to even hint yet at the passing of high summer. It made sense to her to be wearing a T-shirt. Here was where a role model might be useful, Joey thought. Someone to smack her, and tell her to wash and iron her only good shirt, even though she had to wear it to work tomorrow. This was a Woman she was going to see.

That's exactly the kind of advice I need, Joey thought. *Now why didn't I come up with it sooner?* Steve had just shrugged and opined that clothes didn't matter, as she'd be naked soon enough.

That was another thing, the naked. She'd only ever been naked with Psycho Barbie. Joey was sure she wouldn't do it right. There had to be kinds of naked. Satisfaction, though, not guaranteed. She'd managed, so far in her young and pathetic romantic life, to disappoint one girl. Not a snowball's chance in hell, not even with an October Surprise ice storm, that she'd be able to satisfy a woman of Experience. She didn't even know how to kiss, and she'd met a girl that knocked her down, flat out. She dove into it with less than appreciated results. Over the years with Psycho Barbie, she'd learned to kiss like Psycho Barbie wanted. Maybe that wasn't all there was to it. Maybe her learning would help overcome the fact that naturally, she wasn't much of a kisser.

It was deeply, foundationally difficult to feel sexy and powerful when she was taking a bus in a dancing cheese T-shirt to have sex with a woman who, she distinctly saw, was doing her a favor. No real sexual, primal, charismatic animal magnetism there. Just her, just Joey, riding the 20 away from downtown, feeling clumsy, and hungry, and hopeful. That little wagging tail of hope so shocked Joey that she nearly yanked the cord down and stopped the bus. No blood in the ashes of her heart. *Keep your hopes in your pants tonight*, Joey warned herself. No matter the fun of the e-mail exchange, this was still an experiment. *Keep the yes*, Joey reminded herself. *Keep saying yes.* If anything got out of hand, all she would have to do was walk away and call Steve. He'd be there with the cavalry in a trice.

The ride took half an hour on the 20 bus, running up Elmwood toward Kenmore. It was out of downtown, away from Allentown, and against every instinct Joey possessed. She hadn't left Elmwood, Allentown, or the West Side in months. Not since Psycho Barbie kicked her out of their North Buffalo, university-adjacent apartment. Since she, in the first grand, suicidal, bathetic gesture of her fall into despair, dropped out of college to work full time. Joey clutched her backpack strap convulsively. Overnight bag? What the hell? Clean underwear and a toothbrush, done. Okay, T-shirt and socks. Really, how did people learn to do things like pack an overnight bag? Where, at whose knee, did you learn the small social graces of a flourishing and generous sex life?

Two blocks off Elmwood, to the right, side door, upper bell. Joey noticed that both bells read N. Zimmerman. Weird. She rang the bell. The window directly above her head opened.

"Hi, Joey. I'll toss the keys down. Let yourself in."

Naomi tossed, and Joey, hoping for a smooth, single overhand grab, the most insouciant and charming of grabs, ended up clutching them to her belly like a bad receiver. Naomi did not appear to be watching. The door opened on a staircase, so Joey went up. At the top of the stairs was a woven mat with rows of shoes. She took the hint and unlaced her sneakers and left them there, and wore her socks inside. The door was cracked open. Joey pushed through into a kitchen, a bright, sunny yellow kitchen with a faux marble top sunny yellow table. It was Apollo's breakfast nook. Enameled suns in saffron, ochre clay suns with thick snakelike rays haloing, blood orange sun candles, neon plastic sun magnets on the refrigerator holding up hand-drawn childish suns with big feral grins. Joey felt mesmerized and a little unsettled by the plethora of them. This was a woman who could commit wholly to her theme, her quirks, her emotions and gallop with them. It took balls, big bouncing brass balls, to make a kitchen this sunny.

"Are you hungry?" Naomi asked, appearing out of the darkness in the next room.

"Uh, no, thanks, I ate." This was a blatant lie; she'd been too nerved up to contemplate toast. But she was used to eating one meal a day, or at widely dispersed times, with the demands of her job and poverty, eating standing up over a sink, usually.

"All right, we'll get to it, then. Put your bag down next to the kitchen table. No, parallel. Better. Take off your socks, fold them, and put them in your shoes in the hall. Now."

Joey paused, considering. It was different, in real life, Joey noted, thinking of the stables. This was the prelude to a story of some sort, a scene. If she was patient, Naomi would outline her part for her. But could she pull it off, thinking on her feet? Naomi had been kind to her, and warm. Joey felt, absurdly perhaps, that she could be trusted, as a teacher is trusted, to lead the way through new and strange territory. She had something that Joey wanted, that power and assurance. To have the freedom to laugh, and seduce, and move on, like Steve did. To choose to be daring. This was the most daring she'd ever had the chance of being, outside of leaving her hometown. She'd already galloped past her former limits of experience and met an actual Mistress. How many people could say that? Joey felt that her luck had turned, she'd stumbled into a rare opportunity. What if people were shaped by their adventures, as much as shaping them? To become bold, she had to act bold. The adventure in the stables had been a hot, promising one. Plus, she was learning to like saying yes. So Joey went with the moment and did exactly as Naomi asked.

Naomi seemed to read her hesitation. "Remember, you can stop at any time. Say your safe word, and we're done."

Her tone held the touch of warmth that Joey needed. Joey nodded, gearing up her courage. "Okay."

Naomi was dressed in a long black skirt, with a broad patent leather belt. Her white blouse was straining to be proper, tasked with reshaping her fruitful bosom into a starched ski slope of disapproval. The buttons on the neck went nearly to her chin and were surmounted in a white ruffle. Long sleeves similarly debauched into white foam about her wrists. There was no evidence of jewelry anywhere. Her hair was tied back with gusto, the waves and curls as subdued as children before a deathbed. Wire-rimmed bifocal pince nez tilted at the end of Naomi's nose. Before her, clasped like Athena's aegis, was a black leather folder, a black and white composition notebook, and a thin cane rod.

"What do you know about dog training, Jocelyn?" Naomi asked, her voice cold and precise.

"A little, Mistress. We had dogs when I was growing up."

Naomi shifted the notebook and folder to her left arm, and held the cane free in her right hand. "What are the basics of dog training?"

"Your commands have to be clear, they have to know what you want them to do, you have to mean it, or they will be able to hear it in your voice and they'll keep ignoring you. You have to reward good behavior."

"And bad behavior?"

"Punish immediately, so they know what to correct."

The rod dipped and rose, indicating the next room. "Precede me, Jocelyn."

The room was a dining room, but the only furniture was an antique mahogany desk, lit with a single green-shaded lamp. Naomi sat down at the desk. There was no other place to sit, so Joey stood in front of the desk at the edge of the circle of light.

Naomi looked up at her. "Take your right hand and clasp your left wrist, behind your back. Shoulders back, chin up, chest out. Feet straight. This is how you will stand before my desk, is that understood?"

"Yes."

"You will use my honorific after every answer, understood?"

"Yes, Mistress."

"Better. If I have to repeat myself, I get cross. You don't want to make me any more cross than I already am, do you Jocelyn?"

"No, Mistress."

"Good. Then you will listen to every word I say, you will be honest and prompt in your answers, no matter the content of the question. Understood?"

"Yes, Mistress."

Naomi pushed her glasses back on her nose. "Good. We will begin with your student profile."

Joey realized she was being interviewed, within the scene. Her sexual history—simple, a count of one. No history of violence. Moderately good relationship with her family. Cold, formal, symbolic rather than expressed. Everything signified something else, something deeper, but only by inference.

There was a brief review of her personal relationships, with a deeper series of questions exploring her roommates, as if her support system were also on trial. The questions shifted, abruptly, back to more explicit.

Naomi put the book down on the table, walked around and leaned on the desk, facing her. The cane nestled in the crook of her arm. Joey struggled with where to put her eyes. Naomi was taller than she was, maybe five seven to Joey's five four. That placed her, with a modest slouch from the hips, at dangerous proximity with Naomi's restrained bosom. If such a pallid term could convey the swelling, oceanic majesty of those breasts, crashing against the breakwater of the restricting undergarments. Valiant, futile undergarments, for in Nature, all things run to their appointed level, the tides come inexorably into the sea caves. Breasts will run free.

"Do you like attention paid to your nipples?"

"Mistress?"

"Do you not understand the question?" Naomi stood up, and took the hem of Joey's T-shirt in her left hand. "Unclasp your wrist. Raise your arms above your head and leave them there."

With a decisive snap of her wrist, Naomi removed Joey's dancing cheese T-shirt and tossed it on the desk. Joey fought not to cover her chest with her arms. Naomi watched her struggle with the moment. Being exposed before the teacher was excruciating. Joey felt a moment of panic and wondered what she was doing here. How could this woman possibly understand her or what she was going through?

"Do you always wear a sports bra?"

"Yes, Mistress," Joey said. Did this woman expect to find her in lacy bras? Frilly things? Was she unsure of what she was getting? Annoyed, Joey felt like putting her arms down. This was none of this stranger's business.

"Good. Tell me why," Naomi said, walking around behind Joey. Joey stood militarily straight. She felt Naomi's breath on the back of her neck, felt the barely there caress of nails slide down her shoulder, then they traced the slope of her clavicle. The sojourn in the hollow of her throat began.

"I didn't want to develop. I was a tomboy, big surprise. But while I thought of myself like a twelve-year-old boy, my body didn't agree. I had the body of my Scots peasant ancestors, as Mistress can see. Solid, pear shaped, round. Big hips, big tits. Strong. But not lean, not long, not angular. Soft, even over the muscle."

The caress proceeded down Joey's side, slid intimately around her ribs. "Wonderfully so, yes. Continue."

"It's not really pretty, Mistress."

"I want the truth, my handsome girl. Pretty is far too shallow for me. Continue."

"I didn't want a woman's body. It was like a jail sentence; once you got one, all the fun went out of your life. You had to care about stupid things, and not the good things anymore. I was going away, in the middle twilight state of girlhood before the axe falls, when you are still a person and not a woman yet. Not that lesser thing that doesn't get to leave the house, or think, or speak." It is a hard thing to tell the truth. Sometimes, it is easier to do so to strangers. Joey felt the anger of her childhood clenching along her jaw. Could Naomi even understand what her life was like? What emotions she was kicking up? The heat of anger had to be boiling off her skin.

Joey felt Naomi's hand pause at the back of her neck and wait there. The stillness encouraged Joey to be still, and she found her breathing calming. Naomi did understand. When the anger started to choke Joey, Naomi recognized it and backed calmly away from the questioning. Joey felt the memory flare with old, buried pain.

She'd been fourteen when her mom told Joey that she was too big to go outside without a bra, especially playing with boys. Boys were dangerous and not to be tempted, as they wouldn't be held responsible for their actions. Joey's mother brought home this thing from the department store: triangles of flowered fabric and pointy bits held together by yards of wire and elastic, like a Viking chick's breastplate in a cartoon opera. Joey called it a harness and refused to wear it. Eventually she lost and got broken to the harness.

When her breathing was measured again, Naomi spoke. "I'm still angry at becoming a woman, at what it meant, culturally. And I enjoyed being a girl, loved the thought of being a woman. But not what it meant."

"You may lock your hands behind your head. Good. Tell me about your first sports bra."

The physical action gave Joey a chance to move and flex, shrugging the emotion off. She felt a welling sense of security, that Naomi could bring her to that point, and bring her back down. Naomi was paying attention, was being respectful with the power she wielded, like any good teacher. Joey hadn't expected to be taken care of emotionally. It made any physical exposure easier.

"It was plain. It was functional. No flowers, no little bows, no wire, no pointy bits. It held my breasts in, didn't emphasize them at all. It had dignity." Joey was surprised at the strength of the list. She'd never thought about it in detail, but it was right there under the surface. She'd never gotten over being forced to wear a bra. It was one of those things she'd never talked to anyone about, and so thought that she alone had had that experience. It added to her alienation from other women and increased her sense of isolation. "I wasn't a proper daughter. I disappointed my mom in all things girl," Joey added bitterly.

"I'm going to give you an alternate interpretation, Joey.

You were a butch young woman, faced with growing into a body that meant the death of all your hopes and experience. You didn't want to be the kind of woman presented to you as the only option possible. You needed a butch role model, and didn't have any, so you looked at growing up into a woman as a punishment."

"Yes, Mistress."

The pomegranate nails, Persephone's shade, dipped down into the tight valley of the sports bra.

"You are doing very well, Joey. But we mustn't forget that you are here for a reason. You've already committed several infractions for which you will need to be punished. I see everything. You may have gotten away with such sloppy behavior in the past, but I expect nothing less than excellence from my pupils. You placed your bag at a forty-five degree angle to the kitchen table. You wore your socks into the kitchen. You can't answer a simple question: Do you like attention paid to your nipples?"

Joey was now in a much more information-rich environment from which to draw the answer. "Yes, Mistress!"

It was easy to like attention, when the person paying it had already acknowledged herself. Already showed that her emotional state mattered, that it was noticed and responded to. That was unique, in Joey's experience. Psycho Barbie didn't acknowledge or care what Joey's emotional state had been. Naomi made Joey feel seen. There was more here to learn than she'd thought. Not just experience, but skill. Finesse. It allowed her to sink into the sensation, to really feel the fingertips that rolled her nipple back and forth, caressed and tugged.

"These may seem like minor infractions, silly little things, but I assure you, they are not. They are signs of a disordered internal house. My pupils are expected to keep themselves under explicit control, to be aware of the meaning of every one of their actions, and to take pride in their precision and excellence. I am exacting in my demands. Do you imagine that you can measure up to my expectations with this sort of sloppy, disrespectful behavior?"

"No, Mistress," Joey said, trying not to sound breathy. Evidently, she really liked attention paid to her nipples. This did not seem to surprise Naomi, who would stop the motion of her fingertips whenever Joey hesitated in answering a question.

"What is the principle of punishment?"

"Punish immediately, so they know what to correct, Mistress."

Naomi stood up and caressed Joey's face with the back of her hand. "Exactly. You have a good memory, Joey."

Joey beamed at the compliment, then tried to look chastened again.

"I am not here for my health, Joey. It is hard work, running a school. Hard, tense, demanding work. A woman in my position of authority has needs. Relaxation needs. Yet I cannot relax my control one iota, or pure chaos breaks out. Think of the girls. If I don't punish you, immediately, word will get out that I've gotten soft. Soft!"

Naomi thrust the tip of the cane into the flesh under Joey's chin and tilted her head up a fraction. It reminded Joey of the stables and gave her an inkling where the scene was likely to go. That hint of familiarity grounded her.

"Can you imagine what that will do to my reputation, Joey? A woman in my position. Soft. All my carefully built authority, gone. I can't have that."

"No, Mistress!" Joey mourned the loss of Naomi's fingers.

"You don't want me to lose all my authority, do you, Joey?" Naomi whispered, very close to Joey's ear.

"No, Mistress. Punish me."

"That's my clever girl, understanding the greater good. Understanding your personal responsibility. That is how you earn my respect, Joey. Now drop your trousers on the floor."

Joey complied. Nothing had been said about her boxer shorts, and she didn't want to presume, so she stood there with her jeans around her ankles and waited.

CHAPTER FIVE

Naomi had gone back behind the desk and pushed the chair away at a forty-five degree angle. It was as massive as the desk, mahogany, straight backed and stiff, arms padded with maroon velvet rests. It was a chair for popes, for kings. For mistresses. Naomi spread wide her skirt into a pool of obsidian. In her left hand the cane swished and snapped, a vegetable sound of motion and resistance. Naomi patted her knee.

"Come along, then. Step out of your trousers and lie across my lap."

Joey draped herself across the arm of the chair, spilling into Naomi's enveloping lap. Naomi's right arm was beneath her, Naomi's left held out, with the cane triumphant. The crow wings of the skirt spread for her. Joey felt ridiculous, a full-grown twenty-two-year-old butch, sprawling with her ass in the air in a reversed pietà. Naomi should be mourning the slain Joey, but the promised little death was not yet. Premature resurrection? Then the cane cracked down next to Joey, causing her to vault like a salmon up a rill.

"I think five strokes are sufficient to improve your behavior. I am impressed with your attitude and willingness to accept responsibility for your errors. That speaks well of your character. Perhaps everything I am teaching you tonight will not be in vain."

"I sincerely hope not, Mistress." Joey squirmed as Naomi's fingers found her nipple again. This position had its strengths, and Naomi played to them.

"Should I pull down my boxers, Mistress?"

Joey felt Naomi's hand, holding the cane, run across the band of her boxers.

"What is your instinct, Joey?"

"Clothing is protection. So, yes, I should remove them, to show you that I am not protecting myself from you."

"Well done. Remove them. Plus, I like to see the marks of my authority written in red across your alabaster flesh."

Joey now sprawled, nearly naked, in Naomi's lap. She felt less ridiculous when Naomi did not treat her as if she were engaged in anything ridiculous in the least. The internal structure was there in the scene. If she was honest and took the game in earnest, she would be met more than halfway. Mutual belief creates worlds.

"Reach out and grab the arm of the chair. I want you to count each stroke aloud."

Joey nodded, then said, "Yes, Mistress." The anticipation of pain was flooding her. It was nothing compared to the pain itself. It hurt! Explicitly, unambiguously hurt. Not a mote of symbolism, just pain. The stroke of the cane was a line of fire across her ass. Tears formed in the corners of her eyes; she nearly forgot to count the stroke.

"One," Joey said through clenched teeth, fairly certain that she was not a natural sub. The pain was painful, not erotic, and she could feel the same about shutting her hand in a car door. The arousal she felt cooled.

Naomi's fingers spread across the outraged flesh of her buttock, caressing. It mitigated some of the pain. "Remember, you are being punished for a reason. Keep that reason in mind, always, when being corrected. How you react to correction is an expression of your character."

The caressing was lovely. When Naomi's hand went away, Joey was more ready for the fall of the next stroke.

"Two." The pain was raw, but this time, Joey knew in advance how it was going to feel, how long it would last. She also knew that Naomi's hand would follow, sweetly easing the skin, waking up all of her nerve endings. It was the admixture of the two, liquid, flowing together, that did it. There was necessity and art in it.

"Three." The stroke fell, evenly, exactly like the previous two. Tempered strength, measured pacing. A calm, dispassionate caning that gave the impression of concern for her welfare. Naomi, Joey realized through the pain, was taking good care of her during the caning, bringing her up slowly, marching one step up with each stroke.

"Four." The stroke of the cane wasn't as vicious. The force used must have been the same as the others, the measure and rhythm identical, but it hurt less. When the caress came, it was even sweeter. Joey's arousal returned. Naomi's fingers found her nipple again and matched the caress of her buttocks. This was starting to make sense.

"The last stroke will be the hardest. Show me how strong you are."

The stroke was, as she'd been warned, harsh. Joey jumped forward from the impact, fingers white on the chair arm, head arched back in a gasp. The cane seemed to sink into her flesh, embed itself in the muscle and bone. It was only pride that made Joey grit out the word.

"Five."

Then it was over, mercifully. The cane came away, evidently not buried in her flesh but merely resting upon it like a lover. Her quivering flesh was cooled with the broad palm caress of Naomi's hand. The pain receded; Joey was left feeling like she was floating. She was gathered up into a sitting position, lost in Naomi's embrace. It was wonderful.

"That was a hard stroke, you'll be marked for days. I'm very proud of you, Joey."

Joey felt like laughing. Where had this giddiness come from? She was in excruciating pain a moment ago.

"Let's not waste those endorphins."

After, Joey wasn't able to relate how it happened, but suddenly Naomi was out of the chair and she was sitting, her hips forward, with Naomi kneeling between her spread legs. Joey had just enough time to worry, as one does when one first has a new guest between the thighs, about the paleness and girth of her legs. Then Naomi began her march from the inside of Joey's left knee, a circle dance of her tongue, lips, and teeth. There was the step-lively alteration of soft and sharp, amplified mightily by the endorphin high Joey was riding. An inspired, snakelike flick of Naomi's tongue moved Joey from sitting to arching in the massive antique chair. The next stroke tickled more than a little, so Joey squirmed away from it.

Naomi seemed to note this, and her nails scored the insides of Joey's thighs. The bite of pain was sharp enough to pierce the endorphin high. It was balancing, the waves of sensation, never staying in one place too long. Not long enough for a feeling to cloy or become common from overuse. Or for Joey to become settled with it. It had been a spectacularly long time since a woman had touched her with carnal intent. She was young, and in need, and being played like a symphony, and was well aware of it. Being able to identify what she was feeling did not impart magical intellectual distance. She still felt it and had to go through it to find the other side. In some ways this was worse than the caning, Joey thought. That was just getting used to pain. This was sitting, wet, wide open, squirming with bruised flesh on the cold mahogany seat, waiting for an older woman's tongue that might never come. This was harder, trying to look tough and cool while wet and waiting. How do you look tough while in need? Even letting on that you were horny smacked of desperation. She wasn't supposed to feel, and not in that way. Oh, but she did. Naomi had shifted her attention to Joey's right thigh.

It wasn't the need so much as the lack of expression for it. In Joey's freshman year women's studies course, the one where she'd met Psycho Barbie, a feminist theater director came and tried a few exercises with the class, to free up their expression. The exercise was this: with the lights off in the room, everyone had to pretend that they were having an orgasm. It was a vocal exercise—the more expressed, the better. Even with the lights off, however, the protection of darkness was not complete. Light showed through the slats in the blinds, under the door, through the keyhole. Joey noticed something immediately. The girls she knew or suspected were straight and the girls she knew identified as femme, or queer, or not identified at all, were able to do the exercise with little problem. They were moaning, whimpering, rising into howls and full-throated calls of thunderous orgasm, theatrical and enjoying every second of the artifice. They knew enough about how they were culturally expected to respond that they could parody it, play with it, romp a bit.

Joey sat with her jaw wired shut, looked sideways at one of the other more butch girls, furious and ashamed. They had the same response to the stimulus. Not everyone, but Joey wasn't alone in her reaction. This was exactly opposite of what she knew about butch sexuality, about how they could express themselves. Joey was convinced that butches were prized for their strength, their control, their ability to be stone. Not for being able to come loudly. That wasn't an option for her.

The theater director, a self-identified femme woman, was alert to the energy in the room and noticed the reaction. Joey could see that she didn't understand. She brought the exercise to a close, and the class sat and shared about it afterward. Mostly the straight women talked about how easy it was. A femme woman asked Joey and the other butch why they didn't participate. Neither of them, Joey sensed, had an answer they could articulate, but it felt more like couldn't than wouldn't. This wasn't funny, wasn't a place of play and exploration for her, it was deadly serious and it felt like insulting their butchness to the core to ask them to be anything but. Joey felt that butches seldom got to play. They only had one mode of being, and it took a long and often cryptic struggle to find approval for who they were. She wasn't able to just throw that away and pretend to be something else, not without knowing it would be all right. Not in front of Psycho Barbie.

This, with Naomi's tongue, a seemingly innocent touch of wetness that wandered ornately, baroquely over the territory of her inner thigh, mapping the edges of uncharted waters: here there be dragons. Joey wanted the touch like a nun yearned for celestial union.

Naomi's hands framed the chalice, rested in the joint of hip and thigh, stretched-out fingers pressed down, gently but firmly, over her soft lower belly. It felt magnificent, the firmness of that touch, the referred pleasure from the inference, the hope, that the touch might get more explicit.

And it did. The pressure increased. Joey felt her heart drop into her crotch, just from open hands pressing down on her lower belly. Naomi rubbed her cheek against Joey's inner thigh, moving up as she did so. Only her breath caressed Joey now, from inner thigh to inner thigh, passing over the center innocently, casually, without lingering. The hot sweep of her breath was a gift. Joey groaned and felt her hips tilt forward of their own accord, begging for Naomi's attention. Naomi, slyly, moved back a fraction when she felt Joey's hips rise, keeping the distance between them. Joey couldn't keep still for that; she sank back into the chair, despairing. Naomi was playing with her. Never, never would there be relief for the tension that lived in her, always, coiled like a sacred snake at the base of her spine. Mistress had simply woken her, to torture her. Bitch. Fulfillment would never come. Her clit was hard as bone, waiting to be polished. Her lips unfurled like sails, riding the wetness of her internal ocean, now surging onto the chair. Joey had never been so wet in her life. The world began in liquid and would end in liquid. Her ass clenched, relaxed, clenched, with muscular expectance, the marks from the cane scorching. Joey started to believe in God, from the note of her internal pleading. She needed to be begging to someone. God wasn't responding, so she swallowed her pride and started begging Naomi.

"Mistress, please. Please."

Naomi had to lift her head away from her tantalizing to answer, a fact Joey hadn't considered and immediately hated. It was too cold on her skin where Naomi's lips had just been, moving closer to Canaan. "Please what, Joey?"

"Touch me."

"I am touching you." Naomi pressed her nails down, to provide evidence.

Joey squirmed, humiliated, miserable. Naomi wanted her to say it. She'd never said such a thing in her erotic life. Not a very long span, but still. A girl had her limitations. Being shy had always worked for her before. It wasn't working now.

"I need your tongue on my clit. Please, Mistress."

The response was immediate, and nonverbal. Naomi moved forward and very delicately, with the tip of her tongue, flicked the top of her shaft, just behind the hood. Joey wept. She wouldn't live through this. Joey's body slumped away from Naomi, miserable and defeated, on the threshold of ebbing desire. That would never do.

Naomi licked, in a single stroke, from Joey's ass to her clit, plowing through the wetness, rising with the welded-to-her-lips rise of Joey from the chair, as Joey followed that stroke as a nomad follows the sun, snapping in the chair like a docked fish. The orgasm came up and blindsided Joey, yanked her head back, arched her spine, ran with a flush of heat from pussy to heart to brain and back. Naomi, kindly, let her ride it out. This had simply been necessary, before continuing. Joey had been too hungry for too long.

"Oh fuck!" Joey heard herself scream. Her body arched and shook. Her right leg shot out and trembled. Her hands clawed for purchase on the impossible to hold slippery wood. Time split, skipped, rolled to a halt.

Naomi was kissing the wet hair above Joey's clit. She tilted her head to the side. "You've only started coming, Joey. I promised you a firm tongue-lashing."

I like her idea of a firm tongue-lashing. I came, I squirmed, she conquered, Joey thought, before her brain tipped over the edge.

The next orgasm Naomi made Joey work for. No more charity. Now her tongue lavished Joey's outer lips, explored the territory of the inner, measured for future building, danced in the orchards and lit Midsummer bonfires on the hills. Two principles, Joey eventually discerned, were at play. The first: Naomi would go close, close, terribly close, but never touch her clit. The second: Joey was forbidden to come. Both principles were held to with a fervor bordering on patriotism. So Joey lingered, windswept, on the rim.

Naomi brought her up, step by step, and Joey felt like Charlie Brown submitting to hope and running after that football. She knew Naomi wouldn't break, wouldn't compromise, wouldn't let her slide off into ecstasy just yet. She'd been kind; now Joey had to earn kindness. She clenched her teeth, thought better of it, and moaned. Naomi seemed to respond with more attention when she was vocal. Nothing like positive reinforcement. Or inverted negative reinforcement, a wavering reflection in a pool of water. Not yet the good and the beautiful, but moving toward it with each reversal, rising up each time struck down. A body united with mind, singular in purpose. When finally granted the grace of permission, Joey sobbed when she came.

Naomi started to get more broad in her play for the third through fifth, treating everything below Joey's hips as a feast. When Joey's right leg was shaking enough to be distracting, Naomi casually tossed it over her shoulder and went back to work. Joey wished she could take notes, pause and congratulate Naomi on being a mistress of her craft, but she never stopped coming for long enough to speak with coherence. Through it all, Naomi directed the action, Joey was convinced, every twitch of her hands, every thrust of her pulse through her veins, every flush of heat radiating out from her epicenter, her omphalos.

Eventually, Joey collapsed in the chair, boneless, gutted like a mackerel. The pool of wetness that she slumped away from was hers, abetted by a generous helping of Naomi's saliva. A mixed media painting, Joey thought, and giggled. Naomi's head, lingeringly kissing at her knee, came up with a feral grin.

"Did you just giggle?"

"I'm sorry, Mistress. I got carried away," Joey said, trying to sit up straight but sliding on the chair.

"Never apologize for being transported by sex, sweet girl. That is a compliment in any circumstances, and the highest compliment from a butch."

With that, the scene was over. Joey felt it leave, like a dog skittering out of the room. It was funny, how quickly she became attuned to Naomi's signals and could read them, face, voice, body, posture, gesture. Even without a change of costume, the play space was gone. Joey felt a little sad; she didn't know who she was expected to be now.

Naomi pushed herself up, with help from the chair. "Whoo! I am getting too old to kneel on hardwood. Come on, kid, we need a beer." She slapped Joey's knee affectionately and walked to the kitchen. Joey looked around for her jeans and slipped them back on gingerly, trying to mitigate the wetness left between her thighs.

She left the dancing cheese T-shirt on the floor and wandered, wearing only her jeans, into the kitchen. Her legs were still rubbery. Joey leaned against the door frame and watched Naomi, black skirt gathered across her magnificent ass, bend over into the fridge.

"I know I have a couple of beers left in here."

Naomi, triumphant, came out of the fridge with two Labatts. She handed them both to Joey. Joey glanced, puzzled, at them, then got it and twisted off the caps. She handed one back to Naomi.

"How do you feel, Joey?" Naomi asked, then took a sip of her beer.

"Like I need a cigarette, Mistress."

"That's a good thing! And wouldn't you look hot as hell,

standing in my kitchen in nothing but your jeans, smoking. Do you smoke?"

"No, Mistress. Used to."

"What about non-cigarettes?"

"Sometimes, Mistress."

"We'll keep that in mind for the future." Naomi patted Joey's shoulder. "Come on, handsome. Bed. You've had a long night, for an introduction."

"But what about you, Mistress? I mean, I feel guilty with all the attention on me."

"I enjoyed the hell out of myself. It's not always about orgasm. Plus, there is time enough for you to learn to please me. You need to be the center of attention sometimes. Get used to it."

Joey woke in the morning, tangled in a web of high thread count sheets, blinking up at a skylight she didn't recognize. Where in the world? Then it came back to her, all at once, like a dream. Naomi's house, Naomi's queen-sized bed, in the bedroom she wouldn't have anticipated—clean, Spartan, white as a clinic, nearly empty. The antithesis of Apollo's breakfast nook. Naomi was gone, she was alone in the bed that dominated the end of the room. Joey stretched luxuriously under the sheets, until her body reminded her of the limits of mortality. There were still lines of fire on her ass, score marks from enthusiastic nails on her inner thighs, and a lassitude that threatened to envelop her in all her limbs. A mix of soft and sharp, like the aftermath of a marathon.

She slipped into her jeans and spare T-shirt and wandered into the kitchen. The explosion of color was welcome and reassuring, as was the sight of Naomi, in a robe and slippers, at the stove. Naomi heard her and looked over her shoulder.

"Good morning. Want some breakfast?"

Joey nodded. "I'd love some. I'm ravenous."

"Ravenous, lovely word. Sit, I'm making challah French toast. There's coffee on the table in the press."

Joey poured herself a cup of coffee and sat at the cheerful faux marble topped table. It was nearly impossible to be sad in a kitchen this drenched in sunshine. This might be better than antidepressants, come the relentless Buffalo winter.

"After a busy night of destroying Western civilization, I always favor a big breakfast," Naomi said, setting a plate in front of Joey.

"Destroying civilization?"

"I grew up with my grandmother always saying to me, no chupa, no shtupa. No wedding, no bedding. Unrestricted fucking leads to the destruction of civilization, particularly our kind."

"That ignores the Greek contributions to civilization, like democracy and science and theater," Joey said.

"A foolish consistency is the hobgoblin of little minds— Emerson. Once you learn to read, you become a problem, because you can see for yourself how broad and strange and beautiful the world is. Here, try the raspberry syrup, it is to die for. And a sprinkle of confectioner's sugar."

Joey took a bite and sighed. It was marvelous. She respected artistry in food; working in restaurants made her impatient with all the ways people destroyed, abused, wasted chances to indulge in feasting. Not just eating, as poverty had taught her to eat a loaf of white bread and a jar of peanut butter for a week. Feasting. The pleasures, from selecting and combining and arousing all her senses in a culmination of art was a luxury. People who could cook often had other sybaritic tendencies she aspired to. With experience, a full kitchen, and time, she'd love to be able to cook like this.

"Mistress, may I ask you a question?"

"Sure, Joey. More coffee?"

Joey held out her mug, grateful. It was such a coded gesture for her, the offering of coffee. It spoke to her of domesticity, cordiality, concern, friendship. Steve and Kaori communicated with coffee. Psycho Barbie had never, in their years together, made her coffee.

"Yes, please, always. What do you do for a living?"

Naomi winked at her, from above the rim of her own coffee mug. "I'm a librarian."

"Really? You don't seem like one. I always thought librarians were grumpy old women who wore their hair in buns and shushed everybody."

"I keep my bun in a drawer in the Reference Desk. I only put it on for especially hard reference questions. It's like Samson."

Joey looked at Naomi, who kept a perfectly straight face for four seconds before dissolving into laughter. "Right. They teach you the shushing thing in library school?"

"With special exercises in finger strengthening for emphasis." Naomi mimed a perfect shush, finger to her lips.

"You're supposed to look stern. The laughing blows it," Joey said.

"I can be plenty stern, trust me."

"I trust you," Joey said, pushing her coffee cup around. Her thoughts started to walk in circles. She felt physically wonderful. Joey wasn't much good at simply enjoying, or feeling. How did Naomi feel? Had she had a good night? What could she possibly be getting from this?

Naomi put her hand over Joey's. "Not yet. But maybe you will."

Joey looked up. "Like friends?"

"Yes. I hope we are friends, Joey."

Joey shifted, Naomi took her hand back. "You have other friends, too."

"I do. I'm very friendly." Naomi poured more raspberry syrup on her French toast. A drop fell on her hand; Joey resisted the urge to ask to lick it off.

Naomi looked at Joey. "You still have the online personal up?"

"Yeah. I mean, I guess so, Steve didn't say he was going to take it down."

"Good. Have you met anyone else through it?"

Joey tilted her head. "No. It was mostly men, or women looking for a third with their boyfriend."

"Surely there were some actual lesbians."

"A few, I guess. You just stood out."

"Compliment accepted. I want you to leave the ad up. I want you to continue meeting women through it."

"You want me to meet other people?"

"Oh my, yes. It will do you a world of good. I want you to meet them, and have adventures. Then I want you to come back and tell me all about them."

"So we will keep on being friends?"

"You bet. Next Friday work for you?"

CHAPTER SIX

On the way to work later that day, Joey noticed a strange alchemy taking place. Before, she felt invisible, drifting through Allentown like an empty plastic bag blowing down the street. Now she was noticeable. People stopped what they were doing when she walked by, and she could feel eyes following her. It was like Naomi had made her visible, marked her with radioactive isotopes, or fairy dust, or a halo, but where she went, she got noticed. Maybe she had a new bounce in her step, maybe it was the feeling of being happy that radiated from her, but people started to flirt with her.

The old guy behind the counter at the convenience store winked at her and called her girlie; that was weird. But women had started to notice her, too. She had something they wanted. She wasn't blending into the woodwork anymore; she was Of Allentown, one of the denizens of the artist's neighborhood. Joey felt like she belonged, that for this afternoon, these were her streets. Birds were singing, small woodland creatures frolicked in her imagination, the day was a slice of summertime heaven.

She was walking to work, minding her own business, distracted by thoughts of Naomi maybe teaching her how to wear a harness, and it happened. She ran right into somebody on the sidewalk, right in front of the Towne restaurant at the corner of Allen and Elmwood. She immediately rebounded and offered a steadying hand to the person she'd hit.

"Jeez, I'm sorry. I'm a bulldozer sometimes," she said.

The person she'd hit turned out to be a woman, a young woman, who was more kind of smiling at her than looking angry.

"No problem, you didn't knock me down."

"Damn, have to keep practicing," Joey said, snapping her fingers. The girl had black hair in the cutest messy tangle about her shoulders, luminescent golden brown eyes, and a huge grin of amusement. She was a year or two younger than Joey.

"You can run into me again, if you like. Just to get it right."

What had she opened the door to? This couldn't be her, Joey, just walking down the street. Things like this didn't happen to her. She managed not to gape at the girl like a child who had just seen the ocean for the first time. What would Naomi do? Laugh, surely, but also smile like she held some special, secret knowledge; like she knew exactly what she was doing. So Joey did.

"Sugar, if I wasn't late for work, I'd love to." The smile was easy, Joey hoped it had the right note of implied seduction in it. "Another time?"

"Maybe I'll see you around."

"Lucky me." That was the right note of hedonism and longing. She grinned again, and sashayed away. Joey watched her go. Daaamn. Maybe flirting was an art that needed practice. Practice sounded like fun.

❖

It took forever for Friday to come again. On Wednesday, Joey had picked up the phone and calmly set it back down, to convince herself not to call Naomi just to talk. They weren't dating. She didn't do dating. Naomi had a primary partner. Currently, a nameless, faceless partner that caused Joey no discomfort. The partner was an idea, not a reality, just another part of the fairy-tale strangeness of the whole affair. Something that lent Naomi glamour.

The whip of lust drove every sluggish minute on, dragging their heels, reluctant and stubborn as stallions not yet broken to the saddle. It was a characteristic of desire, Joey noticed; good sex encouraged the drive for more good sex. She was far more intrigued and consumed by thoughts of seeing Naomi than before their first Friday. The promise of a specific individual was more tantalizing than the promise of sex in general. The newness of it, the edge of tension that ran along the path to discovery was still there, but the specifics of a person, the territory to map, gave it savor. She wanted to fuck Naomi. She wanted Naomi to be pleased, as she had been. Impressed would be nice, but Joey didn't want to aim too high just yet. She was still learning, still following the magic yes. She would someday be that person, the playful, self-knowing adventurer capable of saying yes and no with authority. She would have experience. She could laugh and romp and not lose her heart. Then she could think about dating, and have enough of herself to spare. Emotion would be her friend, not her master. Not yet.

This Friday, she listened to her own advice and washed and ironed her only good shirt. Five bucks at the AmVets up on Elmwood bought her a good used pair of men's trousers in her size, in a light gray cloth. Joey had stood in the aisle, ties in hand, debating mightily on the presumption of showing up wearing one. That would be too formal, too much like a date, she finally decided, and put the ties down without purchasing. But something about Naomi, everything really, made her want to stand up straight, square her shoulders, put on a tie, and go out. Dinner, perhaps, and maybe a walk up Elmwood so people could see them together, see the unlikely pairing. *That's right, this woman is fucking me. Fuck. I got lucky.* But that was decidedly a date, and wouldn't do.

These were her rules, Joey reminded herself. The rules had been what drove her to the online ad, and fortuitously, Naomi. Naomi, who wasn't single, or interested in dating. There was relief in that thought, though. How could she expect to keep up with her in conversation? How to charm or seduce her? Surprise or inspire her? Joey would be lucky to understand what she was saying more than half of the time, and beyond lucky to have an apt word for any of her thoughts.

She stepped off the bus and adjusted her shirt so it sat perfectly above her belt. Her short brown hair was slicked down, a look Joey reserved for formal occasions. It made her look not unlike a choirboy. The memory of last Friday, Good Friday in her estimation, as that holy day really needed a revamping for the new era, had been gone over in minute detail, reformed into a story so she could tell it to herself, again and again. *I did this*, Joey thought. *This is me, having an actual adventure. Robin Hood and his fairy men have nothing on me. I am Lancelot.*

Eager, she rang the bell. She heard the window open, and the keys flashed like fireflies in the wake of the late late sun. This time, she caught them one-handed. She put her shoes, socks folded neatly, perfectly straight in the hallway. She knew which direction was up. She opened the door. Naomi was in the kitchen, wearing her bathrobe, slippers, with her hair pulled back in a messy bun. Joey's heart not quite sank, more sagged. This didn't look like any fun.

"Don't you look nice. You'll have to change. Your costume is in the bathroom. Your hair looks very dapper." Naomi caressed Joey's cheek, then patted it. "You'll have to mess it up a bit. But not just yet. First, we're going to talk."

Naomi took up the far seat at the sunny table. Crestfallen, Joey took the opposite. Naomi pulled out the black and white composition notebook from Joey's last visit, and opened it. She pushed a finger down lines of handwritten information, then took a pencil up. She asked Joey a few questions about penetration, experience, and desired experience. When the questions ran to toys, Joey hesitated, not having the experience to base her answers on.

Joey recoiled, slightly. "In me? I don't know yet, Mistress. Under the right circumstances, maybe. But I don't know."

Naomi stopped writing and looked fully at Joey. "There isn't a right and wrong, Joey. You are always free to adjust you answers, with time, experience and new information. You have your safe word picked out."

"Rutabaga," Joey said, and grinned.

"Yeah, well, you aren't likely to be calling that out inadvertently in a fit of passion, so I allowed it, but you are being a cheeky little bastard, aren't you?"

"A little, Mistress," Joey agreed.

"You're lucky I like cheeky little bastards."

"Is that why you like butches?" Joey asked.

Naomi smiled and set the notebook down. "Oh, there's some truth to that. I do like a cheeky bastard. I like a swaggering boi. But I love a butch woman with wise, knowing eyes and powerful hands, hands that make you feel safe and cherished just by touching you. Hands that fight and fuck and fix things.

I like the way butches pride themselves on pleasing their partners."

"Where did you learn? I mean, did you learn like I'm learning from you?"

Naomi sighed. "Almost entirely unlike you and me. My mentor was an old-school femme woman, and oh, did she know how to live. Passionate, luxurious, elegant. It wasn't so much the sex, though we were lovers for a time, but just being around her, being allowed to watch how she lived."

"Almost entirely unlike," Joey agreed, grinning.

"Hush. I haven't thought about Maria in years. What a voice she had. Let me tell you, the right word growled the right way at the right time can make you come, just hearing it."

"What's the right word?"

"Rutabaga. There, you earned that. Maria had this theory, culled, as she said, from a life ill and widely spent. 'Butches have a woman's heart in a warrior's body. Femmes have a warrior's heart, in a woman's body.'"

"You believe that?" Joey asked.

"I don't know. Maybe I did, once. It seems simple to me now. Still…I've never scratched the surface on a femme and not found a warrior's heart. I don't think women and warriors are separate categories." Naomi shrugged. "People love us and teach us to the best of their abilities. It's up to us to pick what works and move on."

"I'm not there yet," Joey said, looking down.

"You don't have to be. I love teaching a handsome boi how to become an elegant butch. You'll find out what works for you. Don't be afraid to play along the way." She patted Joey's cheek.

"Play," Joey repeated, dragging the word out, looking at Naomi.

"Flexibility of imagination and a sense of humor are ridiculously attractive. You'll have the girls falling all over themselves. I can see it, it tugs at me. There's something waiflike about you, Joey."

"Waiflike!" Joey protested.

"Women will want to take you home and take care of you. And have you fuck them."

"That's okay, then. I have to learn to be a good lover."

"You're well on your way. Communication. There, I just gave you the secret of good sex."

"Communication?" Joey asked.

"Frank communication." Naomi stressed the former word.

"Wisdom."

"Think about it, Joey. You can't moan 'fuck me harder, Mistress! Spank your little whore, Master!' without knowing what you want, how to ask for it, and how to trust the person you are asking enough to give power to them."

"I begin to see."

"Always ask a woman how she likes to be fucked, before you fuck her. Ask her often, as her answer will change, and every nuance is important. Pay attention to her moods, her internal seasons. How much better, I say, to ask these questions before the heat of passion is on you, so you can flow without interrupting what's happening for you."

"How do you like to be fucked, Mistress?"

"Hard and fast. Clever, Joey. Go change; meet me in the dining room."

Joey wandered into the bathroom. On the sink, folded, was a white garment. Joey shook it out, thinking it a shirt. It was a short white tunic of almost diaphanous cloth. A gold braided belt was sewn on at strategic points. It must be a Halloween piece, some Roman or Greek costume. Joey stripped. The tunic wouldn't be so revealing if she were meant to wear anything else, Joey reasoned, so she tossed it over bare skin. She glanced at her reflection in the mirror. Her hair was still slicked down, an anachronism already in her time, and now setting history out of joint with what she wore in reflection. Joey reached up and scruffed her lovingly smoothed hair into a semi-attractive mess. Making a butch play with her hair after it was done must be a form of torture. Hair was something you achieved, set, and never touched again, Joey thought. She was idealistic.

The dining room had been reset from last Friday. The antique desk was gone. The massive mahogany chair had been camouflaged with a cloth, edged in a golden Greek key pattern, enveloping it. It looked taller, set up on some wooden rises. Several deep rugs were piled, cushioning the floor. Naomi was standing before it. Now Joey understood the bathrobe— it had been concealing this flowing, milky white, thinning to transparent in the soft weave, Grecian dress. Revealed, presented, inescapable were Naomi's triumphant breasts, the sigh of a dress barely accenting the firm, proud nipples. The messy bun was understood, too, as it was surmounted with a high and complicated wig involving black curls, gold wire, and a crowning circlet of laurel leaves. It made a hash of historical style, but it communicated, symbolically, the imperious tone of the scene. Naomi looked down upon her, black eyes flashing. Joey gulped. She had simply strolled into the room; now that entrance might be regretted.

"How dare you!" Naomi hissed, furious and frigid.

Joey dropped to her knees on the thick carpets. It seemed like a good idea.

"When I have a mine slave sent to me, they come clinging to my feet and begging for their miserable lives! And you swagger in as if I hadn't just plucked you from my silver mines, had you bathed, and sent to me. Any other would be trembling so with fear they couldn't walk."

It was easy to pick up this game, Naomi had set it all out for her. She was a slave, a brute from the silver mines, hauled before some lady or royalty. Empress, maybe. That usually meant execution. Yet she'd been bathed and sent to her. That was the key.

"Empress," Joey said, and when Naomi reacted with a small nod, repeated, "Empress, I am a low silver mine slave, beneath your notice. Yet the vast difference between our positions has its freedom. If I am here, I am subject to death, thus I am already free. I know that nothing I say in this life will count for or against me any longer, my fate is entirely in your imperial hands. Therefore, I may speak a slave's truth: though you are as far above me as a goddess, still, I am not a fool. You had me bathed before being sent to you, and in this flimsy see-through rag. You desire me."

"The presumption of what you have spoken merits death," Naomi said, the purple delight pouring like syrup from her voice.

"Then slay me. Torture me. It is still the truth, a slave's truth: the mistress desires the slave." Joey took a heady chance and stood up slowly, deliberately, from her knees. "More. The mistress desires to be the slave of a slave."

"No." Naomi's nipples were lancing through the flimsy dress. That was a good sign, Joey thought, so she went with it. She loved gladiator movies, good and bad, a love she shared and indulged with Steve, and could do a reasonable Heston in *Ben-Hur*, with more than a dash of Yul Brynner from *The Ten Commandments*. She strode to the foot of the throne, stepped up on the rise above Naomi, and seized her gown in her right hand. It tore easily from the shoulder.

Joey embraced Naomi from behind, hands cupping her breasts. The gown was pushed down around her waist. It took some doing to figure out what to do with Naomi's breasts; she wandered off and got lost in the lushness, but circumnavigation saw her to the fore. Joey experimented, circling Naomi's areolas, flicking her fingers across the tips. When Naomi pressed her hand over Joey's, urging her to use more force, Joey complied. Naomi squirmed against her.

"How do you punish lying slaves, Empress?"

Naomi moaned. "I have them whipped."

"I bet you could fetch me a whip," Joey said, close to Naomi's ear. This was dancing on the edge, but the rush was astounding. She hoped she could pull it off. It was like running up a flight of stairs that each only appeared when the last one vanished.

"I can. I'll be right back." Naomi slipped away, trailing her gown. In a moment she was back, small flogger in hand. It was russet leather, glove soft, six bladed, wound into a polished hardwood handle. She walked into the room. Joey shook her head and pointed to the floor.

"Bring it to me on your hands and knees." It was a stretch, and a daring leap. But Naomi shivered, and dropped to her hands and knees. She was on the right track. For all her skill and experience, her ability to control and direct a scene, Naomi responded on the primal level to being in someone else's control. This was where she would find her abandon, Joey thought. So she kept up the dominance. Naomi handed her the whip, Joey used it to motion her back to her hands and knees. "Behold the Empress on her knees before a mine slave." Joey paced around her, thinking furiously. Then she grinned.

"I want you to describe, in detail, exactly how you whip your lowly slaves, Empress. I want to know how to punish you."

Naomi's shoulders were tight, her neck held at an awkward angle. It was the weight and bulk of the wig. Joey saw this and stepped forward to help her remove it. They set it aside, Naomi shook her hair loose. Then they went back to position.

"First, I strip them naked. The whip must be free to fall on all their flesh."

"An excellent idea. Remove your rags, Mistress of the World."

Naomi pulled free of the shreds of her gown. Her breasts, pendulous, ripe fruit: take a pull of life. Reach for them. Suckle.

"Then, illustrious one?"

"Then I would show them the whip, so they would know what was striking them. I would run the whip across their cheek, so that they might feel the softness of the leather."

"I like that. But one modification. Kneel."

Naomi did, pushing herself back on her haunches. Joey held the whip before her face and shook out its strands before Naomi's brilliant eyes.

"This is what will be whipping you." Then Joey reached back and slowly locked her hand in Naomi's hair. She waited a moment, to see if Naomi gave any negative signal, but her reaction was a sharp intake of breath, expectant. Joey had, quixotically, stumbled upon one of Naomi's triggers. She pulled Naomi's head back with steady tension, arching her neck, spreading her shoulders and displaying her breasts. She drew the whip across Naomi's exposed breasts. Joey leaned down and whispered in Naomi's ear. "Describe the whipping, slave of a slave."

Naomi practically purred. "I would concentrate on the ass, on the flanks. Some on the shoulders, but not much. Let their ass and thighs feel my whip, and be stung by it. Each stroke I would vary in intensity and rhythm, to keep them from adjusting to the beating. I would punish them until they wept for mercy."

"You have named you own punishment. Kiss the whip, before I begin."

Naomi took the handle and Joey's hand in hers, and kissed both hand and handle. A final kiss was reserved for the strands.

Joey left Naomi on her hands and knees, not knowing what else to do with her. There were no places to tie her, or chain her, that Joey could discern in the room, nor had they discussed any yet. There were other rooms in the apartment, including a third-floor attic that Joey had been forbidden to go up and see. Naomi had told her that her dungeon was above, and that wasn't part of their play. Perhaps there had been a "yet" attached to that statement, perhaps not, Joey wasn't sure. She'd asked why a dungeon was in the attic, and Naomi had smiled. "Better insulation, better soundproofing, and while my mother is nearly deaf, I have no desire to test that theory by playing underneath her living room floor."

The mystery of the two N. Zimmerman doorbells was answered. Naomi owned the house; her mother lived in the apartment on the first floor. The two upper floors were reserved for Naomi.

Naomi knew how to be whipped. She kept her head down and presented Joey a target of her back, ass, and legs. The flogger was deceptively soft and had a much broader striking area than the cane she'd been corrected with last Friday, so Joey was uncertain how much force to use. She started out slowly, with a single strike aimed at Naomi's lower back. It ended up wrapping around her side and flicking the soft flesh of her belly. Joey corrected for that on the second stroke and found the distance, allowing for the motion of her arm and the deployment of the whip. Once she had a feel for it, Joey began to think of Naomi's body as a canvas, and the whip as a brush. Each stroke was building toward a considered whole. It had to be taken into account, not only as a moment of impact within itself, but also within the larger context of the whipping in total. The effect produced would be cumulative. Using the arc and splay of the flogger, Joey explored Naomi's relationship to pain. The variety and strength of the strokes varied, as she'd been instructed. Joey didn't like the thought of causing Naomi actual pain, gratuitous pain, but she did enjoy the experience of watching Naomi react to the stimulation. Naomi was in some space of her own, rising and falling with the strokes, eyes closed, crying out with the sharpest blows and writhing under the more caressing. It was a revelation to observe. Naomi's voice was thick with desire, even in the sharp yelp of a blow hitting a particularly sensitive spot. If her arched back and flushed skin were evidence, her endorphins would be flooding her system. Endorphins are not something to be wasted, Joey had learned, so she watched for signs that Naomi was reaching her limits.

Trouble was, she didn't know Naomi's limits, or how close to them she was getting, or what to do when they got there. She'd heard Naomi's description of whipping a slave until they wept—in character, or not? Should she keep whipping until Naomi cried? Just a tear, or begging and pleading her to stop? This had all wandered into unknown forest, where there were no paths cut, inch by inch, from the uncivilized ground. The skin on Naomi's ass was already a hash of red, the marks staying after the whip flew back.

Joey's arm was getting tired. The motion was more difficult than it looked, repetition and maintenance of the control being the most difficult. She felt as clumsy as a butcher, when it should be an area of finesse, a light, masterful touch. The distance she felt, the important distance, allowed her to be fully focused on Naomi's reactions. It was the translated reflection of the abandon Naomi seemed to be experiencing; Joey was the means to the transformation, the opener of the way, and in the end, the guardian at the gate.

Naomi had brought her up carefully, when she'd been caned, but one of her instructions for the beating was variation, so no pattern could be adapted to. In the end, Joey felt it was too much to go for the climax of weeping and begging. So she improvised and slipped a full-palm caress between each of the strokes, hard or soft. Naomi recognized the change in delivery, and responded, opening her eyes and readjusting to the mix of sensation. The whipping became less virulent, the caressing more prevalent. It was a slip of the hand, at first, when Joey was looking for unmarked flesh to touch and ran her hand up the inside of Naomi's thigh. She was soaking. What to do next became crystal clear.

She slid two fingers into Naomi's pussy, explorationally, and felt Naomi's entire body react. She bloomed out around Joey's fingers, inviting more. Naomi had been candid on how she liked to be fucked, so Joey complied, and when Naomi accepted three fingers and kept rocking back on Joey's hand, she added another and started fucking her, hard and fast. Naomi, on her hands and knees, with Joey behind her, trying to maintain a grip on Naomi's waist while her ass thrust back onto the moving fingers. Hard and fast. Joey put her arm, shoulder, and back into it, braced her elbow against her hip, curved her fingers together for support, curled them to mitigate nails against tender flesh, and pounded Naomi. Naomi responded by howling, shaking, dropping her elbows to the floor for support while she kept fucking Joey's hand. The first orgasm tore through her and pulsed around Joey's fingers; it hadn't abated before Naomi started grinding on her hand again.

"More!" Naomi groaned. Joey folded her thumb and slid

her entire hand, extended, into Naomi's waiting pussy. Her walls stretched and embraced Joey's hand, allowing it to fan open a bit inside her. Naomi's hips pushed back, her thighs, wet with desire and exertion, tensed. Gradually, Joey eased her fingers closed, broadening out her hand, and started to push against Naomi's back wall with her knuckles.

Naomi didn't just want more, she wanted everything. Joey wanted to give it to her.

"Oh God. Put a finger in my ass, baby," Naomi moaned.

Joey slowed her movement to a crawl. "That is not how you ask."

Naomi shook her head, side to side, then looked over her shoulder at Joey. "Fuck your willing slut, Master! Please, put a finger in my ass."

"Nothing is enough for you, is it?"

"No, Master, I want more!"

"Slave of a slave. You will have it." Joey reached her left hand around to Naomi's mouth and imperiously pushed two fingers in. "Get them wet for me."

Naomi sucked and licked at her fingers like she was sucking Joey's cock.

It was hard to coordinate the motion of both hands, fingers sliding every direction, the muscles in her arms aching, but Joey eventually found the rhythm and fucked Naomi with everything she had. If she couldn't offer a proper whipping, she could try to push her limits with the fucking. But Naomi just kept coming, defying Joey to give her something she couldn't take. When Joey's arm started to flag, she braced it against her knee and kept going. Naomi wasn't done. Her head was pressed against the floor, her mouth open, her arms splayed out, the position of prostration before a king or a god. Yet her hips took the thrusts.

Joey pulled back, then collapsed over Naomi's ass,

exhausted herself. She had taken Naomi as far as she knew how to do. Naomi seemed to understand, and when Joey's fingers left her, she fell over on her side and curled her legs up. It might not have been perfect, but it would do.

Joey threw herself down on the carpets next to Naomi, breathing hard. She wasn't sure what to do in relation to Naomi, who still seemed lost in her own world. Naomi sought nothing from her. Joey reached out a hand to Naomi's back and let it rest there, lightly. After the intensity of the moment, she wanted contact, connection, wanted to take Naomi in her arms. The single hand was all the touch Naomi allowed, as she soon shifted away, then sat up.

"It takes me a while to come back," Naomi said.

Joey nodded, hoping that it looked like she both understood and was at peace with that understanding, but deep down, she wanted to be present in the space she'd helped Naomi achieve, wanted physical contact, stroking, confirmation of pleasure had and enjoyed. She needed something more, but this didn't seem like the time to explore that. Naomi seemed very calm, very slowed down, out of character already. She also seemed like she wanted to talk. So Joey, sensitive to this, stayed alert and kept her eyes on Naomi.

"I should have known that you'd be a thoughtful, reserved, creative top," Naomi said. Joey understood. She was already back in teaching mode, maybe to anchor herself after such abandon. If that was what she needed, Joey could give her that. She had questions. The characterization of herself as reserved seemed odd to her. She didn't feel that she was reserved.

"How can you know a thing like that?"

"I'm a good guesser, from how you carry yourself. Plus, you are always thinking, always watching. Always in your head."

Joey played with the pattern on the carpet, tracing it with

her thumb. "So how do you do it? You were so confident, from the first e-mail. Like you just knew."

"I'll give the secret away. You're bold enough to have knowledge when you claim it. Start out by doing your own propaganda, forming your own myth. Speak of yourself as sexually confident and experienced, and people start reacting to you that way. It is like magic. It's the confidence. If you assume it, people think you really have it, until one day, you do."

"I see." Joey sat up and shook out her right arm.

"Have people reacted to you differently since you put the ad up, since it became common knowledge with your friends?"

"Not so much my friends. They always treat me the same. But I've noticed other people start to react to me, strangers even. The whole world is more flirtatious."

"Or you are. They just reflect back what you are showing them."

"Maybe. I feel different. It could show," Joey said thoughtfully.

"I want you to enjoy it. In fact, I want you to test it. Be open to the approach of whimsy. The next time a woman flirts with you, and you are interested, I want you to come on to her. See where it goes."

CHAPTER SEVEN

Joey took Naomi's instruction. The e-mail she chose seemed innocuous enough at first. Spare, to the point, guarded, but clear in intent. This was a woman who wanted to meet. There was an edge of something Joey caught, music from faraway hills. It tasted of metal, stank of nervous sweat. It came clear when Joey reviewed the e-mail. No return address. She asked for Joey's phone number, but didn't offer her own. She said discreet twice. Probably married, although she didn't mention hubby or ask to let him watch. She mentioned not being from Buffalo.

Joey was intrigued. She wanted to know the woman's story. Naomi had seemed ten times hotter the second time they met, because she knew more about her.

On any normal day, she would not have seen the tender side of noon. Wednesday nights were her shift, and noon was often a lovely, hazy memory by the time she rose on Thursday. Here she was, coffee clutched pathetically in hand, and sounding a bit more whiskey voiced than usual, answering the phone exactly at noon, the time she'd arranged with the cagey e-mailer.

"Hello?" *That sounds a little too Old Man River*, Joey thought, and turned away to clear her throat.

"Is this Jocelyn?" It was a woman's voice, tense and brittle, but a woman's voice.

"Joey. Yes, I am."

"Oh, well, good. Hi."

"You got a name?"

"Joyce."

"Hi, Joyce."

"You sound young."

"I get that a lot." Joey's age had been listed on the profile Steve had shown her. She was new enough to the electronic frontier to not think to lie about it.

"How old are you, Joyce?"

"I'm thirty-one. That isn't going to be a problem, is it?"

"Ah, nope. Not at all. What do you do?"

The chill was absolute in the woman's voice. "I'd rather not get into any of that."

Joyce hadn't had a profile, so Joey was shooting in the dark. She heard the call of the closet, the clenched desperation, in Joyce. Naomi had been ridiculously easy by comparison, taking charge of their meeting from the first sentence of her e-mail. Surprising how much character could be communicated in a few words. Joey got the impression that Joyce was waiting for her to take the reins, so she did. It was what she did with expectations, when she felt them leaning up against her, mute in their need. She listened, and once she'd heard, she acted.

"Just making conversation. You mentioned discretion in your e-mail. Twice. I'm not going to ask you any more questions. I'll just talk a bit, and if you are interested, maybe we can meet for coffee, okay? I'm looking for some fun, some adventure. I'm not out to hurt anybody. You got secrets, okay, keep them. I'm not looking for a date or a relationship. I won't be the love of your life, but if we click, I can be the love of your night."

There was a small exhalation on the line. "Coffee sounds nice."

"Good. Friday, then?"

"Friday. Meet me in the coffee shop in the lobby of the hotel on Delaware near North. You know it?"

"Five minutes' walk from my house."

"I don't need to know that."

"Right," Joey said, tiring of the strain this woman communicated. She was humming like high-tension wires, and it was enervating.

The anxiety tipped a bit and spilled over. "I wasn't sure you would be a woman, when I called. I wasn't sure you existed."

That was part of it, Joey could hear it. "I wonder the same thing sometimes."

"Women never want sex. Not just sex."

"There might be one or two." Joey'd felt exactly the same way, before she, or rather, Steve had put up the ad. It was a pervasive community belief, but not many people actually tested it, to know firsthand. The reflection of the dominant culture's image of women's sexuality got drifted in translation. Maybe women didn't just want sex, but there were a thousand uncatalogued hungers in women that no one named. They felt them just the same. Words were only saying part of what was being communicated, Joey thought. You had to look for the spaces between, to get the full mosaic.

"I'll see you Friday."

Joey was happy to have the distraction. This Friday, Naomi had an engagement with her primary partner, Vic. It had rankled Joey, and stung, after their last session together, that Naomi casually mentioned that she was busy next Friday. This was the first Friday that Naomi wasn't spending with her. She'd gotten used to the pattern, the affection and the sex.

Maybe that was what Naomi was trying to disrupt, or maybe there was no deeper meaning to it, but Joey took it personally. In a mix of wanting to get back at Naomi for pushing her away, and a desire to keep exploring, Joey set up the meeting.

❖

Friday afternoon came. Joey was walking up Allen to Delaware and stepped into the restaurant. Steve was working. It was between the lunch and dinner seatings, so Joey knew she'd find him in the kitchen trying to wolf down a meal of his own before the chaos of Friday night. He waved when she came in, plowing through a plate of pasta.

"Hey," Joey said, hopping up on the counter next to him. The head chef loathed it when they sat on the prep counter, but he wasn't there yet. Steve wolfed down a forkful of pasta with artichoke hearts and black olives. His mouth was half full when he mumbled a greeting.

"On your way to your steamy romp?" he managed to ask, after taking a swig of his water.

"It might just be coffee." Joey shrugged.

"Like that's even possible. You are Casanova."

"Don Juan. Casanova was a librarian."

Steve's eyes lit up, and he pointed with his exclamation. "Romeo."

Joey shook her head. "That went too far. I am not a teenage boy about to snuff it over some chick."

Steve put his pasta down and threw an arm around her shoulder. "Amen and hallelujah. If your resolve starts to waver, picture Psycho Barbie's fac and run screaming into the night."

"Got any plans for later?"

"Kao-chan's coming by after work, and Leela, and we're going out for drinks."

"Who's Leela?" Joey asked.

"This girl who was in the restaurant last Friday. She knew you and I were friends, and she asked me if you were working. I told her no, but she stuck around and hung out after the shift. Kaori came down, and we ended up having the best time going out. If you aren't having your steamy romp, you should join us."

"She asked for me?" Joey ran the name through her memory, but came up clear as water.

"She took a class with you or something. She's kind of quiet at first, but she turned out to be a lot of fun when she comes out to play. Real pretty, striking light brown eyes, black hair, this tall?" Steve held up his hand at Joey's height.

Leela. The name wasn't familiar. What class had they had together? Had they ever spoken? Joey racked her brain, but couldn't recall. During the Psycho Barbie heyday, she'd had eyes for no one else. Little surprise that she didn't recall Leela. Apart from Steve, who had been in her life longer than anyone and was thus able to ebb and flow with the changes of contact and still love her, Joey hadn't kept a lot of friends from college.

"Doesn't ring any bells, but some of my classes were huge."

"Well, anyway, she's coming. Think fondly of us, while you are…coffeeing."

"On that disturbing note, I'm off."

Joey was early to the hotel coffee shop, despite stopping at the restaurant and strolling slowly up Allen, savoring the summer afternoon. It was nearly impossible to be down on a day so fair and welcoming. This would be good for her, as Naomi had suggested. She would be able to go back to Naomi and say—see? *I am an adventurer! I'm not too attached to you at all. I can go sleep with strangers.* Joey shook her head. Perhaps that wasn't the best motivation, but there was honesty in it. She was curious about Joyce, and still in need of exploration. Like Odysseus on his boat, she might take a long, circuitous route home. Pray that the gods were not against her.

She missed going to school. It was the first time that had occurred to her since she dropped out. Maybe she was thawing out a bit. The thought of going back to college wasn't immediately repulsive. For now, that was enough, and Joey set the thought firmly aside. Going out with Steve and Kaori tonight sounded like fun. Leela, too. Joey hated the thought of missing out, but she'd set the meeting and now had to carry it through. There had to be standards. She couldn't become flighty, or ignorant, or careless with other people's emotions just because she was experimenting. She wasn't Psycho Barbie.

It was the hour and the beauty of the day. Not many people wanted to be cooped up inside. So Joey had a feeling, when the blond woman in her thirties entered the coffee shop, that this was Joyce. It would be easy to assign this identity and feeling based on the emptiness of the shop, but Joey thought she could pick out Joyce in a crowded room. She looked in every aspect to be a straight, conservative woman: hair long, straight and pulled back, with a hint of bangs, very proper mid-blue blouse that showed a tiny vee of cleavage, set off by a simple gold cross on a thin chain. Prominent wedding ring, tiny, tasteful earrings. Low round-heeled shoes. Handbag. You could bounce a quarter off the tension she projected. This woman was fighting to the death to appear normal, so much so that she appeared to be a caricature.

I look way too gay for this woman, Joey thought, running a hand through her short brown hair, feeling particularly young and scruffy, like a puppy that had been playing in the dirt. The

T-shirt and jeans didn't help, but she was resolved not to dress up for these meetings as if they were dates. She didn't have the money, and it looked like trying too hard. Artful Bohemian poverty would have to do. She halfway expected Joyce not to acknowledge her.

Joyce did acknowledge her, by picking up her chin, then looking furtively to the left and right. There was no one to observe them, other than the coffee shop staff, who were ignoring them.

"Are you Jocelyn?" Her voice was tight, dry, starched.

"Joey. Yeah. Nice to see you, Joyce. Have a seat." Joey stood up and offered her hand. Joyce took it, with a small twitch of what might have been disdain, or profound discomfort. Joyce sat opposite Joey at the small round table.

"You are young."

"I am. But I exist," Joey said.

"Well, that's good."

"How long you in town for?" Joey asked, forcing conversation. What did she have to say to a woman who wanted to conceal everything, and know nothing? Was there any space for them to relate?

"Overnight. I have meetings tomorrow."

Meetings. Generic. No opening there.

Joyce glanced at the counter.

"You want a cup of coffee?" Joey asked.

"No, thank you," Joyce said primly.

Joey shrugged. This wasn't going to be a warm, fun-filled chat fest. "Right. Small talk over. You have a hotel room?"

Joyce looked at her as if this were more what she expected. "Yes, I do."

"Lead on."

Joyce led her upstairs, walking to the second floor. Her room was near the end of a long, silent hallway. She unlocked the door and went in first. Joey ambled to the bed and sat on the edge. She watched Joyce fuss around the room, setting things down and picking them back up. Joyce seemed lost. Was she supposed to know what she was doing? There hadn't been any spark between them, and Joey got the distinct impression that this woman did not like her. Where to go from here? *This, again*, Joey thought, *would be an excellent time for a role model. I'm in the hotel room, now what?* From Joyce's fidgeting distress, Joey read her own failure. This woman expected an experience Joey wasn't providing. There was only one way to find out if her hunch was right. Joey stood up and kissed Joyce without preamble.

There was hunger, then there was starvation. She was hunger. Then she was starvation. This woman was starving. She grabbed on to Joey like a drowning woman, not caring who she pushed down and stepped on to gobble air a moment more. Joyce closed her eyes fiercely. Her body reached for and clung to Joey's, but her face turned away. It was like she wanted the touch so badly, but couldn't even look at the person touching her. It was unnerving. It was like being in a scene with a partner who couldn't or wouldn't articulate their deep desire, but they expected the script in their head to be read psychically. So Joey listened to Joyce's body. She wanted to be held, hard. She wanted to be swept up and taken, wanted to be able to deny what she was doing, at least in the beginning. Responsiveness would undercut the falsehood of her inability to help herself. It was the loneliest sex Joey could imagine. She knew who she was expected to be, that became clear enough, so she took Joyce by the shoulders, kissed her passionately, then pushed her down on the bed. Joyce fell back, a victim of gravity and Joey's advance. There was no culpability in her need; she was being taken, the question of will aside. Her eyes were sealed shut, clenched. But her body softened and opened and started to reach right back for Joey. Once that wall fell, once Joyce reached whatever internal point allowed her to touch Joey, she clung desperately to her.

If you go hungry too long, it changes you. The habit of tension, of resistance as a daily struggle, stains the entire world. The negative virtue of endurance becomes masochistic. You measure your success not on the presence of happiness, but on the absence of temptation, the absence of desire. It is the path of resignation. The horrible thing, the hair turning white overnight thing, is this: it doesn't work. Resignation is only a part-time coping strategy. If you are still alive, you can only ape death for so long. Your mind can convince your body, for a time, that it feels nothing, that you desire nothing. You can do without want. You can gird your life around with barriers and scarecrows, but want will stroll past your guards and gates. It will happen when you cannot plan for it, predict it, or endure it, and once you want, once you desire, your blood surges and you are alive again. When you live in the desert, you will endlessly crave water.

Joyce was undergoing her own personal resurrection in Joey's arms. It was a sweaty, tangled mess, clumsy and inarticulate. It was also working. Joyce softened, opened, gripped on to Joey's body and gave up control of her own.

It was like a performance for Joey: emotionally removed, careful, and attentive to what her audience required of her. It wasn't an act of passion, more of artistry. She didn't think Joyce would touch her intimately, so she kept her jeans on at first. Joyce, once she had negotiated past whatever stopping point kept her hobbled, seemed very eager to touch her, so Joey shed her last bit of protection. Joyce kept her eyes on Joey's body, but kissed it and held to it as if it were the last female flesh she would ever see. It was intense. Dry intensity, austere, not oceanic. Yet intense nonetheless.

Eventually, Joyce rested her head on Joey's chest, her arm thrown loosely around Joey's ribs, and lay in silence that Joey was afraid to break. Joyce surprised her by looking up, right at Joey's face. The blond bangs were like crushed spider's legs on Joyce's forehead.

"You weren't lying to me," Joyce said, her voice unprotected for the first time. It sounded soft, and broken around the edges, like old pottery.

"No." Joey wasn't sure what Joyce meant, but she thought lying was a bad idea in general, so she could agree to the principle.

"You don't seem like a woman. But you are." Joyce sounded puzzled.

"I am, yes," Joey said. What else was she to be?

"But women don't want sex," Joyce repeated, her voice starting to harden back into enameled tones, looking for conflict.

"The last few hours should give you evidence otherwise."

Joyce pushed away, found her bra and blouse and put them on hastily. "This isn't real. It's something else, set apart from the real world. You don't know who I am. I don't know who you are. We won't be running into one another on the street." Her skirt followed.

"Okay."

Joyce was struggling with something. The clothing seemed to ground her. Joey let her work through it.

"But you're not like a woman, either. You don't want love."

"Of course I do. Eventually. Right now, I'm young. I'm in need of some experience. It seemed like a time to explore," Joey said, sitting up against the headboard. The sheets pooled between her knees. "It's a false dichotomy. You can be interested in sex, like men, or love, like women. But men are interested in love. Women are interested in sex. You can want both, need both," Joey said, fairly certain that she was starting to sound like Naomi.

Joyce shook her head. "You can't have both. Society doesn't allow it."

"I plan on having both someday."

Joyce looked in the mirror, checking the ruin of her hair. Her blouse hung open. Joey could see the white flowers of her bra. She directed her response to Joey's image on the bed behind her. "But look at you. You're already an outsider. You're too gay to do things the right way."

"The right way?" Joey asked, trying to sound neutral, though she wanted to put on her jeans and go. This train wreck of a woman had gotten on her last nerve, and from her immediate resumption of clothing, dinner and spending the night seemed entirely unlikely. It wasn't much past eight o'clock yet.

"The normal way. Of course, it won't matter the same way to you, you're already outside the chance to have it. Husband, kids, home, a secure stable life. A community. Friends, neighbors, church. Standing. Respect. Participation in life. You're young, so it's not so important to you yet. But it will be, soon. You'll wake up, and you'll be thirty. You will be on the outside, still, and you will have nothing. No husband, no home, no security, no children, no community, no nothing. Then what? You're poor for the rest of your life. You're without people. You end up alone. I can't live like that. I won't throw everything good away to be broken and alone in the end." Joyce's voice rose with every syllable. She ignored Joey's reflection and finished by talking to herself in the mirror.

"Right. But you'll come to Buffalo to have sex with a strange girl in a hotel room," Joey said quietly.

Joyce's righteousness crumbled along with her expression. She sat down on the bed and didn't finish buttoning her blouse. She was like a balloon that had been pricked. "I get so hungry for the touch of a woman's body. I wait, months, but it doesn't go away. So sometimes I fail. I fall away from grace."

Joey sat up on the bed and embraced Joyce from behind. This Joyce allowed, sighed, and settled into Joey's arms.

"I wish God didn't hate me," Joyce whispered, her hands clutching at Joey's arms. For a moment, Joey felt a protective tenderness for the woman.

"I don't think God hates anybody," Joey said, kissing her nape.

"That's because you don't feel this way. You aren't filled with this disgusting darkness."

"The darkness isn't yours. You just absorbed it."

"You can't understand what it's like. You live in a city. You know people who live their whole lives as 'gays.'"

"Sis, I grew up in Eden," Joey said.

Joyce straightened in her arms. Joey could feel it. "You did?"

"Yep. Small farming town. I was my parents' only child. I carried all the expectations of the family. I never dated in high school. I was eighteen before I came to college and met a girl I fell in love with."

"What happened?"

Joey hesitated. She could spill the Psycho Barbie story. A month ago, at the least prompting, she would have. But the details just seemed tiring, and not worth hashing out. It could be summed up very easily. "It didn't work out."

"But you are still gay?"

"You think straight women give up dating guys if their first ever boyfriend is a dipshit? I thought that was a requirement for first loves."

Joyce chuckled a little at this.

"Yeah, I'm still gay. And you know what? I wouldn't be straight if my fairy godmother appeared and offered to wave her magic wand and make me het," Joey said, aloud, for the first time. It felt good to say.

"You wouldn't?"

"Nope. I like who I am. My best friend is a gay man. My heart, my mind, my personality are all connected to my body. If I go fucking around with any of that, it's like a lobotomy. It's a taking away of self. I have no desire to be less than. I want a full, difficult, passionate life."

"How did you get to be so strong?"

Joey shrugged. "I have friends. Some of them are gay, too."

Joyce shook her head, accusingly. "You make it sound attractive."

"I'm not a snake in the garden, trying to tempt you. I am just being honest. It makes life a lot easier. You're right, I'm young, and living in a city, and surrounded by like-minded folks. I have nothing to lose. I have the luxury of being out. I don't want to knock you for your choices. I can't know what they've been."

The sympathy seemed worse for Joyce than Joey's silent anger or frustration.

"No, you can't." Joyce pushed away and finished buttoning her blouse.

"Okay." Joey rolled out of bed and slipped into her jeans. Joyce was affixing her crucifix. Joey could have offered to close the chain behind her neck, but didn't. "Guess I won't be seeing you around."

"No." The crucifix was caught in her hair; she struggled with it. Joey closed the claustrophobic hotel room door behind her.

Chapter Eight

J oey walked into the bar with her hair still wet from the shower she'd taken after leaving Joyce. She needed her friends, needed good companionship and distraction, not the memory of the profound loneliness that Joyce had gone back to, willingly. She'd watched a drowning woman, after being given mouth-to-mouth, shove help away and march, grim jawed, back into the sea.

Joey's shoulders twitched at the image. She set the thought aside as she rolled up to the table where Steve was laughing and Kaori was telling a story. Joey didn't recognize the third person sitting with them. She didn't work at the restaurant.

"Hey, guys," she said.

Steve was very happy to see her, in a halfway drunk way. "Hey, stranger! I didn't expect to see you tonight. How was the steamy romp?"

Joey shook her head. "Not worth mentioning. Or maybe, too much mentioning to get started. I need a drink."

Kaori pointed to the woman sitting next to her. "You know Leela, right?"

Leela, that was her name, Steve had mentioned it. Leela looked up, and Joey stopped dead in her tracks. It was the girl she'd run into on the street, the same black hair that fell to her shoulders, impish dimples when she smiled, and eyes that defied categorization, eyes that combined playful mixes of color, but might have been gold, or brown, or both. She was wearing a green T-shirt with white lettering that said Kiss Me, I'm Gujarati.

"We've run into one another before," Joey said, smiling.

"I don't think Joey recalls, but we took a class together. I sat a few rows behind you."

"What class?"

"Psychology, first year," Leela said.

"Who taught?"

"Billings, but he had three TAs do all the work."

"Billings?"

"Five feet tall, bald as an egg, huge glasses that slipped all over his face, and a thick Slavic accent," Leela said.

Joey sat, pulling out a chair between Steve and Kaori, facing Leela. "Oh, right, the chrome dome gnome. He looked ridiculous in that huge lecture hall. There had to be five hundred students. I'm surprised you remember me."

"You doubt my steel trap recollection?" Leela said in mock horror.

"It was a couple of years ago."

Leela smiled, seeming to enjoy the challenge. "I can play this game. You sat in the same spot every day, third row center, and always got up during break to bring a cup of coffee to that blond girl who sat with you."

Joey flinched. She'd taken psychology with Psycho Barbie. No wonder she didn't recall Leela. Psycho Barbie didn't like her talking to other girls. "My ex."

"No need to say more. That will teach you to argue with me, though." Leela smiled at her, then looked down into her drink.

"You're right. I'll never do that again."

"You can, if you like. Just remember that I'm always right."

"So the evening wasn't good? No way. Not for a major stud like you." Kaori put her arm around Joey's shoulders and jostled her a bit. The rough affection worked. Joey grinned, a little. She was back home, after wandering outside the boundaries of life. *Everyone*, Joey thought, *should get to feel like this. There might be fewer wars, external and internal.*

"Were you out on a date?" Leela asked quietly.

"Joey doesn't date," Kaori said.

Steve threw his arm around Joey's shoulders, overlapping Kaori's. "Not our little sexual adventurer. She bravely sails the seas of passion, and puts down anchor in multiple ports. She was 'coffeeing.'"

"Sails the seven seas, like Sinbad?" Kaori asked Steve, across Joey.

"Oh, I like that. It has sin right in it, and that describes you."

"Better than Casanova," Kaori said.

"Don Juan. Casanova was a librarian," Steve corrected.

For some reason, it struck a sour note in Joey's chest, having her cheerleading squad bragging about her adventures in front of Leela. Joey felt a little cheap, a little too bright and flashy, more like tinsel than silver. This stranger wasn't used to them, how they talked to one another, what the hyperbole and bravado were covering. There was an understanding in the trio about the pain underlying the start of this desperate adventure, and the jollity was at the mercy of that pain as a foundation. Joey knew that Steve and Kaori both knew, had seen and lived through, the damage Psycho Barbie had done to her. Without that background, Joey feared she looked like a cad, like a rake.

She didn't want her first impression on Leela being such a poor one. Joey felt the image settle on her, and it jarred. It itched and stung. The loveliness of Leela's expressive eyes—golden becoming walnut brown—dimmed a bit. Joey didn't feel like an adventuring hero anymore. She felt like an asshole.

"I was having sort of sad sex with a deeply closeted Christian woman who disapproved of me," Joey answered, pushing away from the table. "I'm going to get a drink. Anybody else?"

When she got back to the table, Steve had Kaori and Leela in stitches over something that happened during his shift. Joey settled in to enjoy the warmth. She felt a momentary stab of annoyance that Leela was there, but it soon faded when she saw Leela interacting with Steve and Kaori. She was polite, attentive, funny, but didn't talk much. She also didn't make eye contact with Joey for the rest of the night. That left Joey feeling more out of sorts than the incident with Joyce, though she couldn't say why, exactly. It was a relief to think no more about it and finally head home for sleep.

Joey was lying on her back in Naomi's bed a few days later, blinking the sweat out of her eyes and trying to focus. Naomi had been teaching her how to wear and wield a harness. It had been a surprise when she'd shown up for their typical Friday. Naomi had a wrapped present with a huge purple bow on top, waiting in Apollo's breakfast nook for her. In the box was a black leather two-strap harness and her first cock. Naturally, it needed a test run.

Naomi pushed herself off Joey's hips, where she'd been kneeling, straddling Joey. "Definitely getting better. You moved very well with me, even though I was on top and directing the fuck."

"I tried to keep up." Joey wiped a wrist across her forehead.

"That's the spirit." Naomi lay down next to her, propped up on her elbow. "Okay, we've had my surprise. Tell me about your adventure."

Joey felt silly laying there with her cock pointing at the ceiling, like a sun dial. She fumbled with the straps, took it off, and tossed it to the foot of the bed. The condom slid half off. "Joyce? It was kind of sad, really."

"How so?"

"She's this closeted, married Christian lady from some small place in western New York. I bet her name isn't even Joyce. She wouldn't give away any personal information. She was wound tight as a bowstring. Gave off that postal worker vibe, if you know what I mean."

"Sometimes those are the best. They really crack open during sex." Naomi's eyes lit up. It annoyed Joey for a moment. That had not been her experience. The coldness of that shell Joyce kept made it like embracing a statue or a beetle. It had been like agreeing to a conversation, then having to do all the talking. It was an experience, to be sure, but not a passionate one. It was more the sad reflection of passion.

"She didn't crack. She kept herself inside. Wouldn't make eye contact."

"She didn't want to see herself reflected in your eyes. Was she rude to you?"

"Not abusive. Just thought I was too gay to function. I didn't spend the night."

"You sound angry."

"Disappointed."

"What did you expect from her? She's deeply closeted. That has a way of crippling the soul, whether you choose it or not."

Joey sat up and linked her arms around her knees. "I don't know what I expected. Something more like making love, I guess. Some affection."

Naomi watched her for a few moments in silence. At length, she said, "You're not really poly, are you? You're just figuring that out, and it's confusing for you."

"Yeah. I mean, I'm learning a lot, don't get me wrong. I'm grateful. But I'm starting to miss being with somebody more than just in bed."

"That could be good thing, Joey."

"But it's not like how you live. It's just old-fashioned." Joey set her chin on her knees.

"Nothing wrong with that. It's always better to know that about yourself."

"This is just a poly time in my life. I never expected that."

"It's more common than you think," Naomi said.

"I mean, my friends are having a great time with it. It's like I'm a football team or something, and they get to listen to me recount the score."

"You sound bitter. I thought you appreciated Steve and Kaori's support."

The mention of their names surprised Joey, then she recalled she had talked about them in detail to Naomi from the first meeting. "I do. I wouldn't be anything without them."

"Why the tone, then?"

Joey sighed and dropped her head. "It was just running into them at the bar afterward. They had Leela with them, and it made things different."

"Who's Leela?" Naomi asked.

"This girl who's been hanging around with them, usually while I'm off with you or otherwise. We had a class together freshman year. She was there when they were ribbing me about everything."

"Did she say anything?"

"No. She just looked at me. Then she didn't look at me. That was pretty clear."

"But if she was upset by it, she sounds like she handled it well and didn't give you any trouble about it," Naomi said, rationally. It made Joey angry. Why wasn't anybody understanding how she felt?

"By not looking at me? I felt like the lowest thing possible for the rest of the night."

"All because some girl wouldn't look at you?"

"Forget it."

Naomi got out of bed and put her puffy bathrobe on. "Okay. Well, I do need to talk to you about something else."

Joey sat up. "Yeah?"

"My mother is very, very ill. In fact, she's dying, and she may go at any time. My siblings and I are splitting the time at the hospital, but I can't be far from a phone at any time. Plus, when it happens, I want Vic with me. She's loved my mom for decades. So we will be spending our time together from now on," Naomi said, sitting back down on the bed.

This was far more serious than Joey had expected. She blinked, hoping that her panic didn't show on her face. In situations like this, she wanted to be brave and calm, unflappable, knowing. The trouble was, she was young, and scared, and had no idea how to behave. She'd never been here before.

Joey wanted to be someone's rock, be the first one they would have at their side, the last to leave it. Even with Naomi's supposedly decadent, libertine poly lifestyle, there was long-term love in her life. There wasn't, still, in Joey's. So even with not being poly and ending up poly for a time, a season, didn't make her romantic luck any sweeter. It still tasted of vinegar. This was the most inappropriate time to be jealous, to sulk or kick her heels. So Joey nodded gravely, said she understood. *That might be the chief thing this adventure teaches me*, she thought as she caught the 20 back to Allentown. *The art of the graceful exit.*

Joey was working, finishing up the last hour of a busy last seating. They'd turned the restaurant over three times since seven. The customers were hemorrhaging money. Joey expected to bathe in the drops of it herself. She'd been sharp, on, all shift, precise, calm, warm, witty when called upon to be, indulgent above all else. From Naomi's theory, she should be possessed of an ordered internal house, as her externals were flawless. It was quite the masque and empty show. Hollow.

Joey knew her eyes were cagey, her thoughts hid themselves from one another, like children in the forest seeking the witch's house. Why this should be she had no idea. Just because some girl who had been in a class with her once started coming to the restaurant, started hanging around with Steve and even Kaori, drinking at the bar with them after Steve's shift was over, on nights Joey didn't work. And on nights when she did. No reason for Joey to start feeling odd. Approached. In a dignified, stately way, coming up slow, but approaching. Maybe. Joey had never been approached in this way, in the way of a shy person seeking out an extrovert. So she couldn't be sure that Leela even liked her. She certainly did seem to like Kaori and Steve's company, and laughed quite readily with them. She also knew that Joey would be around this Friday night, but usually wasn't. So she was coming by.

Joey's tables had cleared. She was dropping the last check when she saw Leela, leaning on the bar in the front room. So Joey made her way, gracefully, through the remains of the diners and joined her. It seemed strange, to meet in the otherwise empty front room, the fireplace cold, the bar not open. Even the lights were not on. Only reflected light from the dining room found them. Joey stood, hands folded in front of her apron. She and Leela hadn't even talked much, Leela seemed so shy. It was awkward. Why, Joey had no idea. Nor did she understand why Leela made her feel so shy. Faced with her, the words would not come. She reached, and found only a name.

"Leela."

"I wondered why you didn't date. It didn't make any sense to me, someone like you, single. From the time we've spent out together, you seemed like a warm, clever person. It couldn't be from lack of interest. So I asked." Leela looked out of the corner of her eye at Joey. Joey saw the warm, brilliant, tawny Madeira and wanted to drown in it.

"You did?"

"Steve told me about your online ad."

"He did?" Joey felt her stomach try to crawl out her throat. There was no reason for her to feel this way, for her internal organs to rebel. If Leela's next words were condemnation, she would throw herself off the Skyway.

"Yeah, the whole sexual adventure thing you're on right now." That was it. Her tone had been too neutral. Joey readied herself to fall on her sword.

"Listen, Leela—"

"I think it's cool." Leela looked up at Joey, with her head

still tilted down, employing just her topaz eyes. The heat of them left only an outline of Joey, splashed on the wall. "I also decided that you owe me a drink. For the night we met again, though you don't remember. It was weeks ago. You were backing up from some woman who had grabbed your hand, and I was pushing my chair back. You nearly ran me over. I nearly knocked you down, but with a twist of your hips, you were like a deer in motion, free and away. I remembered you from class, but just that little glimpse of you, that night, made me wet for you. I never found you that evening, to tell you that you owed me a drink for flashing before my eyes, then vanishing." She leaned closer to Joey, who stood very still. Her head came up, and her lips touched Joey's. "You're going to tell me where you'll be later tonight now, aren't you?"

Joey nodded emphatically and named the bar. "We'll be there after work."

"I'll meet you there."

It seemed to Joey like hours, though it wasn't twenty minutes, until her shift ended, her cleanup was finished, her staff tipped out, and her clothing changed. She was sitting on a favorite bar stool, next to Steve.

"So what's the story with Leela?" Steve asked.

Joey looked away from the door. "Hmm? Leela? Nothing. I thought she was hanging around with you."

"I saw you talking to her earlier. You guys did have that class together."

"We did, but we never talked. That's kind of the thing. She seems, seemed, so shy. I thought she didn't want to talk to me." Joey sounded puzzled, even to herself.

Steve looked at Joey with great pity, or so it seemed to her. "You do get that she's just hanging around to catch your eye, and she looks at you like she wants to spread you on toast?"

"Yes, I caught on to that." *Tonight*, Joey thought.

"She's kind of quiet, but she's hot. She's got that unexpected thing going on, without the rising background music."

"No arguments."

"Plus, on the nights when you aren't here, she's a fantastic listener. She always asks for stories about you growing up. So sweet."

"Steve, did it not occur to you to mention this to me?" Joey asked quietly.

"You're the professional hedonist these days. I figured you were saving her for later or something. I couldn't imagine that you would miss it. It was obvious in a sun rises in the east way."

"And Leela is the sun."

"I think she really likes you. In an I'll be nice to you way, not an I'll suck you dry and leave you to rot way. Plus, according to The Book, she is smoking hot."

"That's just what I have to be careful about, Steve. She is hot. But it's not my clit that responds first when she's near me. Second, sure. It's like there is a conversation we are about to have, and what she says will change my life. But I don't know if I want my life changed just yet. I'm managing okay right now."

"Right, your heart is an impenetrable fortress."

"I do what I have to do. Love is like lava. Pretty from a distance, but you don't want to be standing in it." Joey saw the front door open.

Leela looked for them. It was lovely to see how uncertain she looked until she saw them and lit up. Then she was smiling, striding across the floor, and Joey was patting a bar stool for her.

"Glad you caught up to us. We're the Love Haters Club tonight." Joey lifted her drink.

"You love haters?" Leela asked, swinging onto the bar stool next to Joey.

"No, we hate love, as an emotion. Or concept. Or personification as a little boy with a missile weapon," Steve said.

Leela thought about it. "That would make you the Hate Lovers?"

"That is now officially too confusing, and my head hurts. We stop. New topic." Steve put his drink down and spun around. "Better yet, cute boy dancing. Bye-bye."

Joey lazily waved to him, then leaned on the bar and looked ahead. Leela studied her profile.

"What can I get you?" Joey asked, glancing sideways at Leela.

"Oh, you don't really owe me a drink. I thought that was the way to approach you, get your interest, by being brazen," Leela said, smiling.

"Wow. Now I need a drink." Joey signaled the bartender.

"You really didn't get that I've been flirting with you?"

"There goes my carefully built rep as a major stud."

"Okay, new topic. Former topic, even, which seemed to be hating on love. That seems harsh," Leela said.

"Yeah, well, love sucks," Joey ground out with conviction.

"All love?" It might have been philosophical interest, but Joey thought she detected a note of actual pain in Leela's voice.

Joey leaned forward and punctuated every word with a dip and chop motion. "The romantic kind. The Paris in the springtime shit."

"I've never been in love, like I've never been to Paris, so I'm not sure if either one exists. I'll have to visit first before

I can say." The tip of Leela's tongue appeared, like a rare songbird, winged across her upper lip, and was gone.

"Dude, I hope you got the money to get to Paris. It beats the other thing," Joey said, wondering after the tongue.

"Did you seriously just call me dude?" Leela's smile became the room to Joey.

"I'm such a guy." Joey flexed her biceps. If it were possible to flex ironically, she did so.

"You are the most beautiful guy I've ever seen. In a really tough girly way." Leela poked her in the ribs.

Joey rolled her eyes. "Shut up."

"Way to take a compliment."

"You're right, that was bad. Punish me." Joey hung her head.

"I'm free tonight."

"I live down the street."

"You have roommates, though. I don't." Leela looked toward the dance floor, and Steve. "I live in Allentown, over on Cottage." Right around the corner from Days Park, practically in Joey's backyard. Leela sounded matter-of-fact, not at all flirtatious and daring. Joey matched her tone.

"Let's go."

Leela took the dare, showed her hand, and took Joey's, on the way to the door. It had not been at first sight, though the pleasant warmth and interest, the spark, were there early. It might have started when Joey noticed how Leela watched her face when she spoke, how Leela's gaze would start at her eyes, drop to her lips, and return, as if so much of Joey was important to take in all at once. It was a moment, innocent, hidden between two other more self-conscious moments, just when Leela made a self-deprecating joke, then glanced down. When her treasured eyes, her topaz eyes, her Madeira and tourmaline eyes came back up, they weren't guarded yet. They were open and tender, and Joey read such a want there that it ran all through her in stricken response. A bell didn't ring; she rang. She wanted Leela, hard.

CHAPTER NINE

Leela's apartment on Cottage was at a V from the house where Steve kept his apartment. Their backyards merged in an arrow point.

"Weird. I could probably see in your window if the light were just right, and I were leaning the right way," Joey said, when Leela opened the downstairs door and went up the stairs.

"You'd have to know I was here to look for me," Leela said, unlocking the door at the top of the stairs.

Joey whistled. It was one of the treasures you could find in Allentown, tucked right in with houses that groaned and leaned in the wind, as Steve's did. It was a charming 1870s Victorian, one of the old Painted Ladies, green and purple and gold, but faded, showing signs of superficial neglect. Inside, it was a dream. The entire second floor was practically a single-room apartment, save for the bedroom and bathroom. The granite countertop of the kitchen ran the length of the open space that served as living room, dining room, and hallway back to the bedroom door. The wood of the walls was blackened by tar in spots, displaying rough grain and cut, all under a new coat of something warm as diluted honey. The whole place glowed. A wood stove, against a copper-backed wall, dominated the left of the great room on the way in. Leela left her shoes there. Joey did the same.

The floors were hardwood, the walls half timbered, meeting exposed brick on the way up to the pointed roof, beyond the exposed beams.

"The wood was from the original building. When my landlord was restoring it, he saved as much as he could and used it decoratively. I think it has great character," Leela said.

She noticed me looking at the wood, Joey thought. "It's an amazing place."

"He went crazy restoring it."

"I love the cast-iron stove and copper wall. There's nothing like a fire."

"There's a fireplace in the bedroom," Leela said, then turned to hang up her light jacket.

Joey wandered around, gaping. It was stunning. Outside, it looked not too different from Joey's place, but inside it was an enchanted find.

"How did you ever get this place?"

"I know, right? Just lucky, I guess. It's an Allentown Christmas miracle!"

Joey laughed. There were two couches dividing the living room space, set with their angles in response to the kitchen. Joey sat on the couch facing the distant iron stove.

"So what will you nickname my place?" Leela asked her, from the kitchen.

"Pardon?"

"It's what you do, you and Steve and Kaori. You're always renaming things, people, places. The world gets brighter and more colorful when you three get your hands on it." Leela was pouring two glasses of red wine.

Joey took the glass of wine, feeling the flush creep up the back of her neck. Is that what they did? "Honey walls," Joey said, impulsively.

"Would you like a fire? I can open the windows, it's a little cooler out tonight. It's almost fall."

"Isn't that extravagant?" Joey asked.

"Ah, but also beautiful. Why not have something beautiful?" Leela walked toward the wood stove. Joey was hard-pressed to argue, watching her walk. Why not have something beautiful?

When the fire was dancing in reflection on the copper wall, when the wineglasses were halfway empty, when Leela was seated next to her on the couch, knees touching, Joey felt a profound sense of vertigo, a spinning on the lip of the abyss. It was like roller-skating on razor wire, with greased wheels. It was about to get bloody complicated in her life, and she could feel it. Leela was still holding her wineglass. That became a problem when Joey kissed her. Leela made a soft noise, a gasp, against Joey's lips, and kissed her back, pressing into her. The glass tilted madly, spilling a few drops on the floor. Joey reached out, took the glass away from her, and set it down on the floor. It let her see Leela's expression for the first time.

"You look so sad," Joey said, pulling back. Leela's eyes were swimming, rip your soul out wide under brows bowed up, eyes of sadness or longing that ran over into pain.

"It's not sadness," Leela said, pulling her back in. Joey came forward, slowly.

"It looks like it would be worse than kicking puppies, if I stopped." Her lips were very close to Leela's.

"It would be much worse. Think of the puppies, and kiss me."

Joey kissed her, fell into her, melted. It wasn't like anything she'd experienced. Leela was so open with her, so intimate it almost hurt. She was vulnerable in Joey's hands. Joey could feel it. It forged Joey's will never to let anything hurt her. Everything Leela did, every moan, every wide-eyed look, every squirm of her hips went straight to Joey's heart. There was no armor to be had against Leela. Joey wasn't fucking her so much as moving toward orgasm with her. She held Leela close, pulled in, while Leela's hands clutched at her shoulders, moving closer. Leela's jeans were down around her hips, Joey's hand was inside. Leela was surging against her fingers. She was so wet, Joey slid right inside, just the tips, held back by the angle and the clothing.

There was no permanence. Every moment birthed the next moment, and the awareness of the passage of time, measured by the passage of her hands on Leela's skin, became painful for Joey. She never wanted to stop caressing Leela, but once her hand moved even a fraction, then the caress was done, brought on to the next. She couldn't hold Leela. At best, her hands could move across her skin in a distinct moment in time. To touch her, truly touch her, would require everything beyond the skin, the intangible and ethereal, the way to the soul through the flesh. The character, the personality of Leela pushed so far out beyond her physical bounds that Joey was swimming in it, frolicking as in a river, hidden in a forest, bathed in moonlight.

It took some doing to get out of their clothing, an arm here, a leg there, while still connected at as many points as possible. Eventually, they were naked and entwined on the couch. Joey watched the firelight, reflected from the copper wall, splash on Leela's brown skin, shading everything red.

Leela was embracing Joey. Her arms were vines, wrapping around Joey; her breasts met Joey's, kissed and pressed together in a never-ending field of motion, of sought-for union. Nothing about Joey was lacking; all the fault lay in the distance between them, which Leela strove mightily to overcome. Joey was not allowed to remain distant, controlled, objective, uninvolved. She was as lost in the heat and the struggle, the pain of realizing that they were separated by gulfs when wound about one another, tighter than secrets. Her fingers pushed deeper, her wrist was held by Leela's hand, not to guide but to connect, Leela's desire wetting both their fingers. It wasn't contact enough. Leela pressed her upper body against Joey's, threw her legs around Joey's waist, and locked her ankles, drumming her heels on Joey's lower back. She kissed Joey, her free hand keeping Joey's head tight to hers, rambling in Joey's hair, scratching at her neck. Always, always pulling her in.

When she came, she gasped and closed her eyes, then, with effort, opened them again and stayed locked with Joey. It shook Joey to the core, the trust, the intimacy of being with her while Leela came. Her legs trembled, her stomach shook and rolled, the muscles taut under the soft flesh, shifting, as Leela coiled under Joey's hand, her lips parted, her eyes wide. Still shaking, Leela pressed her forehead against Joey's and her eyes drifted closed. Then Joey was kissing her eyelids, her cheeks, her lips, while Leela clung to her. The intensity of it was greater than the orgasm.

"I can't get close enough to you." Leela struggled against the limitations of the couch, of the separation of their flesh, against the flesh itself. Even lying under Joey, their bodies in embrace from head to foot, it was not enough.

"Again."

"Again?"

"Again."

❖

In the morning, Joey woke still on the couch, with Leela sleeping half on top of her. It was early; she could hear birds outside. Sunlight crept across the floor in phalanxes. Joey blinked a few times. Leela's head was pressed up against her neck, in the hollow of her shoulder. She turned her head slightly, it shifted Leela just enough that she woke.

"Good morning," Joey said, hoping she sounded romantically deep voiced, not like she'd been working in a coal mine for decades. Leela smiled at her, eyes still half closed.

"It is, isn't it. Did we really sleep on the couch last night?"

"We did," Joey affirmed.

Leela sat up in stages, moving off Joey's body. She wiped a hand across her chin.

"I hope I didn't drool on you."

"No more than necessary," Joey said gallantly.

Leela giggled.

"Did you just giggle?" Joey asked.

Leela shook her head. "Ridiculous. I would never do such a thing. You're hearing things."

Joey popped her head over the back of the couch like a prairie dog. She squinted at the ziggurat her jeans made, piled a dozen feet away. Her boxer shorts were halfway under the couch. She fished them out, slipped them on, and went in search of her other clothing.

"Any morning you have to look for your underwear is a good morning," Joey opined.

"I'll embroider that on some pillows and set them on the couch," Leela said, fetching her own pants. Impulsively, Joey went over and kissed her. Leela dropped her pants.

"I like that reaction," Joey said.

"But we can't go have breakfast pantsless," Leela protested weakly.

"We could try. Steve's big on the whole down with pants lifestyle. Maybe we can get him to join our new movement."

"Do you want to call Steve and Kaori? We could all have breakfast," Leela suggested.

"Sure. But I doubt Steve will be out of bed at this hour. Or Kaori."

"Joey, it's noon."

"Oh," Joey said, sheepishly. Her time sense was entirely skewed.

"You have to work this afternoon, right?"

"Yeah."

"But we have time for breakfast?'

"Sure." More than likely, they had plenty of time.

Joey called her own apartment, and Steve answered, sounding world weary.

"You must be joking, it's barely noon."

"Wanna have breakfast with me and Leela? Is Kao-chan up?"

"Oho, it's you! Kao-chan, I have Joey on the line," Steve yelled, without covering the receiver. Joey heard Kaori's bedroom door slam open, and her run into the living room.

"Will she tell us what happened with Leela?"

"She wants us to have breakfast with her and Leela."

"Guys? I'm right here."

"Oh, well, heck sure and all, we will, meet us on the porch in five."

Leela came out of her bedroom, changed and groomed. It made Joey aware that she was, so far, wearing only her jeans.

"They both are up for it. We're likely to get some questions, so be prepared for rudeness and boundary issues."

"I can take it. Anything I should say about, well, anything? What are we doing here?" Leela's tone was light, playful, but Joey got very still.

"I hope we're friends, Leela."

Leela walked past and slapped her on the ass. "You bet we're friends, Joey. Now get moving."

Like friends, they walked up Allen to Days Park, like friends, they talked a bit, easily, not finding the awkwardness Joey had halfway expected. Joyce, well, conversation had been a disaster, pre and post coital. Naomi liked to talk after sex, but it was teaching or questioning, not conversation. Her authority, even when amorphous, was present. Joey felt a little lost in conversation with Naomi, and most often was cast in the listener role. It was easy to do, and she wanted to have Naomi decant her knowledge, but Joey's own instinct after sex was play, to romp, to cuddle and be silly. Naomi was very serious. Joyce was already gone. Leela seemed to share her instinct. Conversation was light, dancing, one word running off after another without effort, each new idea sparking another three. It was the only application of multiplication Joey could remember. They passed an empty parking lot by Nietzsche's, passed the closed kink shop and bar, passed the open liquor store on the corner. Broken Miller Lite bottles made a nest of glass, catching the afternoon sun. A paper cup blew by. The line was forming for the free lunch at the Friends of Night People storefront. In the U-shaped run of grass in the center of the park a dog was playing, running after a ball, a living image in the vampire wasteland of Allentown the day after.

"This is one of my favorite times, when the street of bars starts turning back into a neighborhood," Joey said, looking around.

A man was pushing a shopping cart full of plastic garbage bags around the curve of Allen where it became Wadsworth. In the garbage bags were cans and bottles.

"I know. See that guy? His name is Claude. He's part of the ecology of Allentown, sweeping through after the nights of tourists and debauchery, feeding off the remains of the revel," Leela said. She nodded to the man, then walked over. "Morning, Claude."

"Afternoon, Miss Leela. Got a cigarette for me today?"

"Sure."

Joey watched as Leela fished in her pocket and pulled out a half full pack of cigarettes. She tapped one out for Claude, then gave him a second. "For later."

Claude thanked her and went on his way.

"I didn't know you smoked," Joey said as their paths uncrossed.

"I don't. I just carry some to give away."

"He didn't ask you for money."

"Who, Claude? No, he wouldn't. He was working; you saw the cart. He won't ask for money if he's working."

"How do you know him?"

"I've lived in the neighborhood a while. You get to know folks. Claude worked for Bethlehem Steel for nineteen years and left just before it was shut down. His back gave out."

"I'm impressed."

"What, that I talk to Claude? Please don't be impressed with simple human decency. Let me do something worth impressing you, like save a basket of kittens from a burning building or something."

"Maybe you impress me without having to try." Joey's hand brushed against Leela's as they walked. She caught Leela's fingers and held them as they approached Steve's house.

Steve and Kaori were waiting on the porch, Kaori standing and waving, Steve slumped boneless against the wall like a cooked strand of pasta.

"Ohayo," Steve mumbled.

"More konichiwa by now, but close enough," Kaori said, and smiled at Leela. "Good morning."

"Ohayo, Kao-chan." Leela returned the smile. Joey looked at her.

"Where to for breakfast and/or lunch?" Steve asked.

"Well, we do have to be to work in an hour and a half. How's the Towne?"

"I wish we had more time. I'd take you to Amy's Place," Leela said, playing with Joey's fingers. This was not lost on Steve, who grinned wolfishly.

"All the way to North Buffalo? Out of Allentown? That doesn't sound like Joey at all."

"Ignore him. Amy's sounds great. Rain check?"

"Sure."

The walk to the restaurant was easy, and Joey managed to avoid any blatantly rude comments from Steve by giving him the death stare whenever he caught her eye and grinned. It would still be coming, certainly, but it was held off for now. They took a table by the window, Joey and Leela on one side, Steve and Kaori on the other. Steve had been pleading on his knees for coffee before Joey hauled him to his feet and tossed him into his chair. The waitress was a lifer, one who knew them and put up with them as fellow restaurant workers. In return, they tipped outrageously, for the continued good service and karma.

"Why is it that restaurant workers like to eat out so much?" Leela asked, watching Steve and Joey fight over the menu.

"I have a theory on this," Steve said. His momentary distraction allowed Joey to steal the menu from him.

"Expound away," Leela told him, grandly.

"You would think, wouldn't you, that anybody who worked in a restaurant would be sick to death of them when not working, yes?"

"With you so far," Joey said, not looking up from the menu.

"But we spend so much time in restaurants, that becomes our model for the world. That's how we become imprinted."

"We're like ducklings?" Joey asked.

"Then we are cannibals, because you made a lovely crispy duck a few months back," Kaori said.

"I'd be a cannibal then, too. I like to eat my own," Leela said.

"You sure do, sugar." Joey patted her leg.

"Don't get distracted. Stay with me. Our model for the distribution and consumption of food is a commercial one. The service model. Once you absorb that idea, then you can easily adjust to the pleasures of having someone else cook, bring you food, and clean up," Steve finished, pleased with himself.

"You sure we're just not enjoying an extended adolescence and are in need of some mothering?"

"God knows you are," Steve said to Joey.

Breakfast finished, the wreckage of souvlaki and coffee making a necropolis of its own in the center of the table. Joey tilted her chair back and sighed. They'd made it through breakfast without the questions she'd been expecting. She did have to kick Steve under the table, but only once, when he was making faces at Leela when she wasn't looking. It was like hanging out with friends, not like a typical morning after. But there were morning-after symptoms, like the way Leela rested her hand, lightly, on Joey's thigh while leaning on the table to talk to Kaori or Steve. The way Leela would sometimes take Joey's hand when speaking to her.

"I wish you didn't have to go to work," Leela said to Joey.

"Yeah, me, too."

Steve took Kaori's hand and looked longingly into her eyes. "Oh, Kao-chan, if only I didn't have to go to work!"

"Steve, oh Steve, if only you didn't date boys!"

"Or you date Ken!"

Joey glared at Steve, furious, but Leela laughed and dropped Joey's hand. She seized Kaori's, taking her away from Steve. "Kaori, Kaori, Kaori, you must know I am only hanging around to catch your eye. It is you, and only you, that I so tragically love."

"Leela, Leela, Leela, your name is too much fun to say, though I love Ken."

"It is fun to say, isn't it? Lee-la. Leela. Leeeeeelaaaa."

"Good tongue warm-up."

Steve faced Joey and burst into song. "How do you solve a problem like our Leela? How do you catch a dyke and pin her down?"

"Carpe dykem. Seize the dyke."

"That's enough, the waitress is giving us a look. Let's leave with some of our dignity intact."

On the walk home, Leela asked, casually, if they were all going out after work.

"Not likely, after last night," Joey said.

"You could stop by my place, if you like."

"Maybe I will. Yeah, just for a bit."

Leela smiled at her, squeezed her hand, then sauntered away down Allen. Steve threw his arm around Joey's shoulders and watched with her.

"Nice view."

"You have no idea, Steve. You have no idea."

CHAPTER TEN

Work flew by. Joey had no recollection of the shift the moment she put her street clothes back on and walked out the back door. She hadn't spent the evening thinking about Leela, or thinking about anything deliberately, but occasionally her memory would toss up a scent, an image, a feeling, and Joey would be transfixed. The moment would pass, she would breathe again as if everything were normal and go on serving.

The way to Leela's place was already familiar, only a few steps off her normal route. There she was, in front of the faded beauty of the house, in front of the door at the bottom of the stairs. It was too late to ring the bell, Joey thought. What if Leela was sleeping, and she disturbed her? That wouldn't be good. Maybe she should just knock lightly, to be able to say honestly that she had, just in case Leela got angry that she hadn't dropped by. But that didn't make a lot of sense; Leela did not seem likely to get angry about anything foolish like that. Like, say, Psycho Barbie might have.

Now would be an excellent time not to be thinking about Psycho Barbie, Joey thought, stricken. Not while standing on Leela's doorstep, hand extended for the knock. Why was she even coming up? Coming up like a vampire out of the grave,

Steve would say. Joey pulled her hand back. The door opened inward.

"Hi," Leela said, softly, looking at Joey from a three-quarter angle. Her hand stayed on the door, gripping it.

"Hi." Joey felt dumbstruck. Had Leela been this ravishing ten hours ago? How did she even walk down the street without ending civilization?

"I left the door unlocked so you could just come up, because I thought you might think it was too late to ring the bell. But then I thought, you wouldn't have any way of knowing that I'd left the door unlocked, so you might just knock, and I didn't know if I'd hear the knock. I mean, most people ring the bell, right? So I came down to leave a note that I'd left the door unlocked. But then I thought that was too much like asking criminals to break in, so I threw the note away and just came down to crack the door a little and hope you were that observant." This was blurted out without true pause for interposing breaths. *Leela might be nervous*, Joey thought. *Maybe she'd feel better if I tried some humor, lighten things up a touch.*

"I would certainly hope I was. But this is me we are talking about, I didn't notice you flirting with me until you ambushed me."

"Is that what it felt like? An ambush?" Leela said, leaning back, pain making inroads in her voice.

It was remarkable, Joey thought, how very quickly she could go from experiencing nigh religious awe to feeling like she'd just murdered a child.

"No, no, nothing like that, just as a strategic, military attack kind of thing."

"Attack?"

"Well, you did kind of sneak up on me." This was, Joey

thought, only getting worse. Leela looked like she was going to cry.

"Dear Lord. Please let me start again. Hi. You look gorgeous, and I would love it if I could come in for a while."

"Are you sure?" Leela asked, pretending to shut the door on her.

Joey set her hands against the door, holding it open. "Yes. I'm sure."

Leela threw the door open. "Then it's your own damn fault. Abandon hope, and all that."

Joey followed Leela up the stairs, an enviable position on any night, but particularly on this one, when the embrace of her trousers left nothing to Joey's fervent imagination. Despite being reprimanded endlessly by her mother when young, Joey looked with her eyes and with her hands. Leela gasped and turned on the step, suddenly facing Joey. "You think you can come here, make me feel low, then just play grab ass and be forgiven?"

"Not exactly like that, no. My hands have a mind of their own. And your ass is a work of art."

"Poetry. Sheer poetry. You do know how to woo a girl."

Joey leaned up slightly and kissed her. It was a slow, thorough kiss, unhurried and uncompromising. In its way, it was a historic kiss, the first time Joey kissed Leela exactly this way, with the emotion at the front, not the desire. It was the start of a conversation they would spend the night having. Desire came and visited, but emotion got there first.

They kissed from the door to the kitchen, all along the grand granite countertop, past the living room and the potential gravity of the brown couch, on back, along the wall, to the door at the end of the apartment, the bedroom. Joey hesitated, even pulling away from Leela's lips.

"Do you want?" Joey asked, glancing at the door.

"I want," Leela said, kissing her again. The door fell open under the press of their bodies.

Honey walls was a better nickname for Leela's apartment than Joey had known. The walls of Leela's room were the same reclaimed wood as the living room, but buffed and polished and finished to a warm honey brown glow. An occasional dark-framed picture punctuated the amber of the room, as did the ebony frame of the print above Leela's bed. The bed itself was covered in pulsing orange, bright and brilliant, with a handful of scarlet pillows tossed like drops of frozen blood across the ocean of the bed. They stopped kissing long enough for Leela to show Joey around the room, gravely as a child, serious. *Here, the elements that intimately make me up. My self-concept, my presentation, the things I yearn to have around me when I close my eyes, and when I open them.* There was beauty everywhere, color everywhere.

The print over Leela's bed was of a blue-skinned young man, garlanded with flowers, playing a flute and surrounded with young women gazing at him adoringly. The title was *Krishna and the Gopis.*

"Tell me about that," Joey said. She stood behind Leela, embracing her as she looked at the print.

"One of my favorite stories. Krishna, the blue-skinned fellow, is a god. He's the beautiful young man, the flute player, the passionate lover. He once lured the young women of this town, all gopis, or cow herders, to come play with him in the forest."

Joey kissed Leela's ear and murmured, "Uh-huh. Tell me more."

Leela opened her eyes again and focused on the print. "He inflamed them with desire, so they would vault over all societal restrictions. They burned with passion for him."

"I like this story."

"He multiplied himself, so he could make love to all of them at once."

"This is my favorite story." Joey traced the shell of Leela's ear with her tongue.

"He was playful with them, hiding their clothes when they bathed in the river, playing word games and love games, always bringing them to the union of the carnal and the spiritual. They are famous for their unconditional devotion to him."

"Best. Story. Ever." With each word, Joey placed a kiss on Leela, each one a jewel for the necklace. "Leela?"

"Uh. Yes?"

"How do you like to be fucked?"

"Repeatedly. By you."

The same question, posed many wet hours later, elicited a slightly different response, proving Naomi's belief in the variety of nature. On the way to the latter answer, Joey discovered how many and various were the ways of interpreting Leela's response. For example, just because she wanted to be fucked first on her back, thighs triumphantly wide as eagles' wings for Joey to nestle between, resting there precariously, teetering on the edge of flight, didn't mean that she wanted that an hour later. There might be great variety in movement, intention, focus, drive, to each of the moments, episodes, scenes within the frame of the night, jewels on the necklace. Infinite variety in finite bounds. The blue-skinned god would approve.

Joey lay, sticky, soaked, Leela's brown thigh thrown carelessly across her hips. Still they kissed. Leela pulled away to take Joey's face in her hands.

"You're amazing."

"No. We're just good together."

"That, my dear Joey, is to damn with faint praise."

"Frankly, my dear, I must give a damn, then."

"Love me again."

"Love you?"

"For tonight. Be the love of my night."

There was work, then there was Leela. Joey favored one over the other, to the point of madness, for the rest of the week. She had to be pried from Leela's lips to make it home in time to change and run to the restaurant. Oddly enough, she saw as much of her roommates as ever. She and Leela took meals with them, went drinking after work with them, kept a circle up. On their third night together, Leela asked Joey if they could spend the night at her place.

"My place?" Joey asked, puzzled. "You know I have roommates, right?"

"Sure. Who would love to see you, I'm sure, and who are very good company. What's the matter, Joey, afraid to let me see you in your own habitat?"

"Nonsense. Ridiculous. Absurd. Expressionist. Okay, fine, come over after my shift."

Joey found herself at home, after her shift, pacing, and waiting for Leela to come by. Steve had worked the same shift, and so was awake. Kaori was a little sleepy, but the promise of a visit from Leela, and the potential drama, was worth it.

"This is historic, I can't miss it. This is the first time you've had a girl sleep over," Kaori said, looking at Joey.

"This isn't a sleepover. I mean, it might be. But Leela is a friend. She's just coming over to hang out."

"I'm sorry, my impeccable English must be slipping. I thought you called Leela your friend."

"She is my friend."

The doorbell rang. Joey went to the stairs, but Leela was already walking up, having discovered that they never locked the downstairs door.

She met Leela halfway up the stairs. "Hey."

"Hey."

"I was going to put a sign on the door, then lock it, then unlock it, then take the sign down, but I got lazy. Which is good to remember; we never lock the downstairs door. We have nothing worth stealing."

"I'll keep that in mind."

"You look stunning."

"Do go on." Leela hugged Joey, stepping up.

"I love that shirt. I can't wait to see it at the foot of my bed."

"You are a cad. A bounder and a cad. We should go up."

"Why?" Joey asked, kissing her.

"Kaori is watching us from the top of the stairs and grinning."

"Yeah, you're right. Better go up."

Steve had a bottle of wine, coincidently, open on the coffee table, with four glasses set out. "Oh, hi, Leela. Wine?"

"Sure, Steve. Hi, guys."

"A day without Leela is incomplete, wouldn't you say, Joey?"

"Doubtless."

They all sat around the coffee table, Joey and Leela on the floor, Kaori and Steve on the couch. The wine flowed, the conversation skipped on after it. Soon Leela was resting against Joey's side, casually. Soon after that, she was within Joey's arm, leaning against her side. No one seemed surprised. It was natural and easy. Then the doorbell rang.

Joey felt her blood run cold. Who in the world was

stopping by after midnight? Who didn't know that they never locked the downstairs door, unless it was someone who'd never visited before?

Steve stood up and stepped over Joey and Leela to get the door. It was awkward, but no one seemed to want Joey to go near the door.

"Probably a wrong number. Or a kid playing pranks. I'll go see."

"When a kid plays pranks, they ring the bell a bunch of times, then run away giggling. This doesn't sound like playing," Leela said.

There were sounds of voices, coming up from the well of the stairs. Edges of conflict, rising tone. Then steps, and Steve was back up, looking flushed with effort and frustration. "Joey."

"What?"

"Someone would like to see you."

"Well, why in the world don't they come up?"

"You'd better go down and see her."

Leela watched this tennis match between them and caught on sooner than Joey did. She leaned away from Joey's body, then moved out from under her arm.

"No." Joey said, to the dawning idea, not to any person yet in the room.

It couldn't be Naomi; Naomi had sense about boundaries. She would certainly call. Maybe Joyce? No, Joyce didn't want anything to do with her, once she came and went. Joyce had never known where she lived. That left only the unthinkable.

Joey stood up, glanced at Steve and Kaori, then went down the stairs.

Psycho Barbie was waiting on the porch, looking out at the park. The streetlight showed her blond hair as a silver net. Her lip curled in profile, moved to disgust by the view; she turned and found Joey already standing there. Facial gymnastics covered the initial emotion.

"Joey." She sounded happy. That made no sense to Joey.

"Hi. What are you doing here?"

"Is that any way to greet me? You would think we'd never been friends."

Joey managed not to say, *We never were.* "What brings you to my doorstep at midnight?"

"I was out in Allentown, and I know this is your territory, so I thought I'd drop by. I knew where Steve lived, and I knew you worked till midnight, so you would be up. You know, I stopped by the restaurant the other night, and Steve informed me that you were out on a date. Good for you, for getting back out there."

"Right. Well, it has been seven or so months. You want to come up?"

"Not really. Why don't you come out with me?"

"Come out with you?"

Psycho Barbie stepped closer to Joey, who could smell the liquor on her breath. She'd been drinking and likely had struck out at the bars up Allen or around the corner on Main, so she sifted the bottom of the barrel and came down to Days Park. Joey wasn't sure if she should be impressed with Psycho Barbie's chutzpah, or angry at her presumption.

"Come out with me. We used to have fun, didn't we? I could use some fun."

They had had fun, in the earliest of early days, when Psycho Barbie first approached her and Joey was stupefied into compliance with anything she said. Psycho Barbie looked good, dressed to the hilt, made up, blond hair like a royal flag on her shoulders. She tilted her head when she smiled, a move Joey well remembered from the moments when Psycho Barbie was determined to get her way by being charming. Combined with a wrinkle of the nose, an engaging gleam in her blue eyes, it worked nearly every time. Certainly, it had always worked on Joey, who hastened to comply with Psycho Barbie in a good mood, often to forestall a worse one. She felt the historic compliance on her very lips, automatic as a salivating dog. She knew what Psycho Barbie wanted, therefore she knew what she was supposed to do. It was simple, had always been simple. A need leaned up against her, demanding, heedless of Joey's own desire or impulse. But she'd been practicing saying yes, gathering experience, so she could have and defend her own desires.

"I can't. I have someone upstairs." It surprised her as she said it enough so that her smile came on the heels of the words, dawning slowly. She'd said no to Psycho Barbie, and without elaborate preparation first. It hadn't been the most terrible thing she'd ever had to do, it hadn't wrenched every muscle and fiber of her being out of joint with the effort. She hadn't bled, crawling forty miles over broken glass and barbed wire. She'd simply wanted something else.

Psycho Barbie's eyes got round, then narrowed to slits. Her smile was an aggressive skinning back of lips from teeth. "Oh, really? Same date?"

"Different."

"You are becoming the big new thing around town."

This last was said in Psycho Barbie's warning tone, a sweet, light, and pointed acid beaker of a tone. The only way to meet that was to refuse to recognize it. So, with a dizzying bravado, Joey refused to be called to heel. This was just another joust, a sparring match, a verbal playground like her talks with Steve and Kaori.

"Yep, a legend in my own time. Well, good seeing you. Have fun tonight. I should be getting back up."

Upstairs, Joey leaned against the doorway. Steve, Kaori and Leela's eyes were all on her. She met Steve's.

"She wanted me to go out with her," Joey said, incredulously, compelled to first share this with the one person in the room with enough history to understand how deep that emotion ran.

"I know! Why do you think there was yelling before I came and got you?"

"Was it Psycho Barbie?" Leela asked.

Steve and Joey answered simultaneously. "Yes."

"So what did you say? Did you take my advice and punch her?" Kaori asked.

"No, Kao-chan. But I did say no. I told her I had someone upstairs."

"You did, huh? That's sort of like picking me over your repellent ex. That's almost a compliment, Joey." Leela smiled dazzlingly, making the compliment seem much grander and more genuine than her voice gave away. It made Joey's knees feel weak.

"I know! You're so welcome." Joey beamed and set her hands on her hips. "I wonder, can you stumble into virtue?"

"If you're stumbling, baby, go on, baby. It's working," Steve said.

Joey sat back down and held her arm out. Leela nestled back into her side. Joey almost died from the sweetness of it. It was too soon to think about that, so she attributed the feeling to her unlooked-for triumph with Psycho Barbie, and grinned at Steve and Kaori with multiple sources of pleasure.

The wine was gone down in its red tide, lees clinging to the sides of glasses, joy settling down into a warm glow, the siren song of bed calling. Kaori was nodding, but Steve was still up, talking to her as her head drooped. Joey caught Leela's eye. There was still the pretense that this was just a visit, a drop by after work, casual, no need to assume spending the night or anything like that. The glow in Leela's eyes was stronger than the mellowing joy, and it sparked an answering fire in Joey's. Sleep was the furthest thing from her mind.

Joey stood up and stretched theatrically. "Well, good night, kids."

Leela, grinning slyly, did likewise. "Night." No more need for pretense. She walked toward Joey's bedroom, leaving Joey to follow after.

"Are those spider's legs?"

"I'll explain someday. Watch your step down."

The room was large and ran down to a door that opened on a small balcony. There was no closet. Originally, it was meant to be other than a bedroom, but Joey took what she could find and worked with it. A standing, rather anemic metal rack held hangers and a few shirts, including her good waiter's shirt and backup. The bed was a mattress and box spring sitting on the floor, weakly embraced by mismatched sheets just inches too small. The pointed roof ended in shadows and cobwebs high above. Exposed beams bisected the white space. Now that she looked at it as a host, an entirely new role for Joey here, she felt ashamed.

It was a room of poverty and hunger, putting a game face on having nothing. When she came home at night, she fell on that mattress and welcomed sleep. It didn't matter that the walls were blank and cardboard boxes still sat along the walls, like a warehouse or barracks. Comparing it with the light, color, and beauty of Leela's bedroom, or the elegance of her apartment in general, Joey felt her stomach turn over. There were good reasons she didn't bring anybody home, beyond having roommates. She didn't have anything to bring them to. What was it about Leela that made her forget that, momentarily?

It was too late to keep Leela out, she'd gone first down into the room and had already looked around. Joey felt a spike of misery.

"It's not much, I know."

Leela was staring at her bed. There was only one pillow. "Is that Bakka-neko? I wondered where he was." Leela marched to the bed, and started petting the large cat, currently curled into a ball on the pillow. He woke, blinked at her, then unrolled so she would have more cat to pet. His snowshoe paws extended and flexed each toe, claws out, curling them into the pillow as she stroked him.

"He's a total slut," Joey commented, glad to have something to talk about other than her pathetic room.

"He's adorable. Besides, everyone reacts this way when I pet them. It's embarrassing, really."

"That is true. I've been there."

"You have a little more dignity than he does."

"Mighty kind of you to say."

Leela was now roughing Bakka-neko up with full body strokes. He stretched out, luxuriating. As soon as he did, Leela scooped him up and carried him, upside down and not quite sure of what was happening, toward the kitchen. "Very nice to meet you, Bakka-neko. Good night." Leela deposited him on the tile and shut the door to Joey's room.

"Man, that was cold, waiting till he was all into it."

"I prefer to think of it as an enjoyable distraction, with a graceful exit attached. He needed to go be in the rest of the house for the night. Unless you want him to watch?"

"I've never had to think about that before, but no, I suspect not."

Leela smiled at this, shyly. "For real?"

"For real. Never had anybody here." Joey held out her hand, Leela took it and they sat on the bed.

"If you think I'm going to be all sappy and emotional about that, well, you're right."

"Careful," Joey said, pulling her in close. "No big emotion. One night at a time, right?"

Leela kissed her in reply. The shabbiness of her room no longer mattered; the indignant meowing Bakka-neko was putting up under the door didn't matter. Leela was still wearing clothing, and that mattered and had to be corrected.

"Why are you still wearing this?" Joey said, pulling on Leela's shirt.

"Because you haven't taken it off me yet."

That makes sense, Joey thought, pulling it away from Leela's arms and tossing it to the foot of the bed. It was a lovely shirt, pale coral in color, and looked particularly fetching there, artistically adding a drop of color to the subdued slate blue of the blanket.

Chapter Eleven

Leela pushed Joey down on the bed and straddled her, on top of the discarded coral shirt.

"Oh my," Joey said mildly.

"You are my prisoner," Leela growled, splintering off into giggling.

"I am the prisoner of MC Giggles."

"Hush, I'm dominating you."

"Dominate away." Joey folded her arms behind her head, enjoying the view.

"I need a more commanding costume." Leela sprang up from the bed and surveyed the room. A grin tore across her face, and she seized Joey's good white work shirt from the hanging rack. The black apron was snatched up as well, along with a belt. Leela pulled the white shirt on and buttoned the bottom three, leaving the front gaping from the spread collar to the waist.

"That's commanding my attention," Joey said appreciatively. "But aren't you missing a few buttons?"

"That's for the heaving bosoms. There have to be heaving bosoms in this genre," Leela said, lashing the belt over the tail of the shirt.

"Heave on, fair maiden."

Leela took off one of her earrings and left the right one, a medium-sized gold hoop, peeking through her sable hair. "Captain."

"Captain Hook?"

"Captain bell hooks. I'm a feminist pirate. And you are my prisoner. I and my fierce cutthroat crew sank your ship, innocent convent girl, on your way back from the convent school on the mainland, where you are being raised in virginal seclusion by nuns." Leela tossed the black apron over Joey's head, in approximation of the nun's habit. "Now you are at my mercy."

"Pirates, eh?"

Leela struck a swashbuckling pose, hands on hips, eyes flashing, head thrown back as if facing a snapping wind. A grin of devilment played about her lush lips. "What, you mean to tell me you never met a nice Gujarati girl who wanted to be Errol Flynn?"

"No, but when I think about it, it is really hot." She looked Leela over, head to foot, and felt her breath catch. Joey clutched the apron under her chin. "Heavens! Whatever shall I do?"

Leela straddled her again, earring flashing, smile lit like a bonfire on the beach on a tropical night. "Submit to me, convent girl. I will ravish you with my piratical lusts!"

It was easy to play with Leela, light and effervescent. It just sprang up naturally from their normal interaction, no clear demarcation between moments. Joey thought Leela was kidding, just larking about, but when Leela pressed her shoulders back to the bed, she did so with a force and authority she hadn't displayed before. She was clearly enjoying being Captain hooks. This was a new situation for them. Joey played along, both thrilled with Leela's adoption of power, and apprehensive about the potential for things to go wrong.

"I must resist you! The sisters would never understand if

I gave in to ravishment from a pirate. Even one so striking as Captain hooks." Joey struggled back to a sitting position.

Leela cocked her head. "Then I will use my nautical knowledge to tie you down." She glanced around the room. "Got any rope?"

Joey shook her head. "Best I got is that belt, and shoelaces."

Leela unhooked the belt and drew it off. "This will do. Your wrists, convent girl."

"What are you going to tie me to? My bed's just a mattress on the floor."

The leather ran through Leela's fingers and she contemplated. She looped the belt around Joey's wrists, binding them clumsily in front of her body. "Tying your wrists will be enough. You'll succumb to my charms, and then I'll have you truly bound."

"Mother preserve me," Joey said, in what she hoped was a helpless enough tone. Her wrists slipped in the belt. Leela took the end of the belt in her hand, a lead, a leash, a method of control. It brought the strap up tighter on Joey's wrists. Leela then leaned forward, slowly, insolently.

It was a masterful kiss she pressed on Joey, possessive, willful, concerned at length with her own pleasure. From the shallow corners of Joey's lips, to the tracery of the thin path of the upper lip, to the suspicious plumpness of the lower, seized between Leela's teeth as if irresistible. Joey was pressed back, taken, overwhelmed, left panting as Leela pulled away.

"I've wanted you for a long time."

There was no theatrical tone there, no indication that this was gilded emotion, carnival emotion, a costume put on for play, to be casually tossed aside at a whim.

It was an admission that didn't sound acted at all. It was therefore dizzying, extra sharp, intense, pulled in and thrust away all at once. Joey felt the floor tilt. She wanted Leela to stop, to adopt immediately the stilted diction of play, the oversized splash of feeling. She wanted Leela to never stop, it was that sweet and sharp.

"How can that be, with you a fearsome feminist pirate, and I an innocent convent girl?"

The gold and brown eyes regarded her. Would the tone now change, the wind shift, the edge be backed away from? Rather than back away, Leela leaned in, until Joey could feel her breath.

"Pirates are great romantics, you know. It comes from all the freedom and plunder, living outside the law, answerable only to your own will. It is easy to believe in getting carried away, when you carry away for a living." She leaned Joey down on her side, till they lay facing one another, bodies touching all along their length. Leela's hands roamed over Joey as she spoke, Joey's stayed tied.

"Once, when I was on pirate vacation—"

"Pirates get vacation?" Joey asked.

"Yes, and union wages. I was on pirate vacation, just checking out new ports and things. Pirates love to walk around on land, in disguise of course. I happened to pass by a low wall that sheltered an orchard. It was a fair day, and hot, so I vaulted the wall and sat in the shade of the apple trees."

"Pirates love apples?"

"Pirates love shade. The orchard belonged to a nunnery. I could see that convent school was letting out, and the girls were spilling down the steps. There was one girl who paused on the steps in a dazzling halo of sun, and I was lost. My heart melted into my boots. I wanted to throw myself on my knees before her and swear I would renounce the piratical life, if only she would be mine."

"Describe this paragon."

"Handsome. Strongly built, good shoulders. Yet her face was of a surpassing sweetness, a questioning always about her, as if the world was something to be puzzled out. A gentleness of spirit, a tender heart, all revealed to me, in the way she attended to another of the girls, showed her devotion and deference in small gestures."

Joey felt her heart slip its strings. "Why didn't you approach her?"

Leela shook her head, sadly. "It wasn't time yet. I could see that she was bound up with the other girl, a simpering fool who hung on her arm. I would have to wait."

"Pirates have long memories."

"I waited. Now you are mine, and I will see if the promise of your sweetness was true." Leela rolled over on top of Joey. The eagerness was matched now with more tenderness, as if the virginal convent girl were in fact under Joey's skin. In some ways, she was.

Conflict raged in Joey, knocking her heart back and forth between her ribs. Her clothing was gone, tossed around the margins of the bed. Leela's leg was between her thighs, urging them open, Leela's hands were everywhere. The scene was set, her part outlined for her to accept or reject. It was an easy story to follow. She'd been taken before; Naomi enjoyed doing so. But she'd never given herself. The distinction was not lost on Joey, who, thankfully restrained and annoyingly restrained, had to stay at Leela's mercy. This seduction was more patient, more hesitant than Naomi's whirlwind approach. It sought her response, and paused to look for it. With Naomi, Joey knew that she'd learned how to let someone else be in control. Leela didn't want her to just let it happen, she wanted it offered to her, the abandon, the surrender. Joey would have to come to her, and give herself up.

Joey knew she'd sought to learn how to say yes. It was her

journey, her adventure, the dark forest to the witch's cottage. "I submit" is not yes; "I will endure" is not yes. Only the full and passionate acquiescence of open arms, open hands, open thighs, open blood is yes. The peeled-back heart, fibers, and steel is yes. Only that giving in conquers and exalts the one surrendered to. That yes leaves the beloved as caretaker and guide, into whose hands, in full trust, you must relax.

It was possible, though her wrists were bound, to put her arms around Leela's neck. The positions of their bodies mirrored one another. Joey put her lips to Leela's ear. "Yes."

"Yes, as the convent girl, or yes as Joey?" Leela asked, pausing.

"Whichever works."

"You can be her. But you can always be Joey with me."

"Yes, as Joey."

Later, she wasn't able to say how it happened; it was seamless. One morning, Joey was waking up on Leela's couch, under her. Soon they were having breakfast with the whole gang. Then there was work, and quite naturally, going out after work. If Leela stopped by to join them, well, wasn't everyone happy to see her? She was neighborhood. If they all happened to walk home down Allen Street together, feeling the summer thinning and starting to bleed out into autumn, it made sense to laugh, and joke, and hold hands, to be young and almost free. If Leela's apartment happened to be her eventual destination on most of those nights, well, who minded? Everyone was having a good time. Joey in particular. She'd never spent time with a girl who enjoyed her friends, who fit in. It was very enjoyable to watch Leela socializing with Steve and Kaori. It was an enchanted time, a honeymoon, even, but life would interfere eventually. Dangerously enjoyable, though Joey wouldn't think that yet. Five days passed, and she was still spending her time largely with Leela. Naomi would call, or someone else, and Joey would have to have all the conversations she was trying to avoid. Naomi didn't call, and Joey felt guilty about being relieved. She didn't want to see Naomi exactly yet. That would mean that she had to examine what she was doing, put names to actions and possibly, emotions. Joey wasn't ready for any of that.

A night off seemed like a good idea. Joey couldn't recall if it was her idea, exactly, but it did seem like a good idea. She must have agreed to it, if she hadn't suggested it. It would give her some time to clear her head. Good idea, if the night weren't moving in molasses, making action impossible and thought labored. Why was everything so slow? Maybe it was all the running around she was doing, Joey thought. Maybe that was what was exhausting her. Yet, until tonight, she hadn't felt exhausted. Adventure, as she had discovered, was its own reward, an elixir as habit forming as any in the mortal world. That was not to say that she could no longer enjoy her own company, Joey thought. Of course she could, hadn't she always been alone?

That thought cut a little close to the bone, so she set it aside. Her early life had been one of silence, the silence of small agricultural towns, the silence of an empty house, the silence of restrained disapproval from her mother, the silence of indifference from her father. Maybe that was why, when released, she never stopped talking. Why she and her friends expressed themselves in language as constant and varied as the chatter of birds, the call and response from the pulpit, the lilt and shriek of children at play. Steve, who had not been an only child, had been highly verbal since his early years, his small piping voice making his mother initially delighted, and later, when the tone didn't coarsen and the theatricality deepened, nervous. By the age of five, his brothers tried to beat the silence of masculinity into his flesh, but Steve, then and now, would not be told what was right and wrong when he plainly could see for himself.

When the moment had come to run, they chose it without the elaborate preparation of prisoners, they simply grabbed at it and fled. Talking the whole while. It was a time for dramatic speeches, never leaving one another behind under enemy fire, we will die in one another's arms bravado and spit. All the eighteen miles, one for each year endured in Eden, they ran, to Buffalo. Both landed at the university, Steve studying pharmacy, a five-year program promising him a good job at the end. Along the way he picked up a beautiful Castilian Spanish, thanks to attention from Carlos, and various luxuries and toys from admirers he'd never be able to buy on his own. He gathered a sense of the trade value of his beauty, greater and more golden the farther he got from the wheat fields. If love, to Steve, seemed like a fool's game and a trap, well, perhaps it was the Eden of his youth that still haunted him. Whatever his distaste for it, he enacted the physical forms of love with expertise, and enjoyed variation in excess.

Joey had gone the opposite way. Starved for love as she had always been, she developed a taste for it that was as immoderate as Steve's, but ran in the opposite direction. She wanted to fling herself off Niagara Falls, without the barrel, for her first broken heart. She wanted to give everything she had and several years more. She wanted to be consumed and devoured. So she chose love with teeth, fast love, love without moderation, the first love to wander by and express want. Joey was helpless in the face of want, having so many years become the repository without relief.

Joey often wondered if their strange reflection of one

another, the inversion of their expression, was just the same desire and hunger filtered through both the ache of their childhood and the prism of gender. Would Steve, who she knew to be tender and great hearted, have gone her way, valuing the relationship above all sense, gone masochistic as she had if awash in estrogen? Would he sacrifice and tear away his own flesh as unworthy, if he'd been female? Would her hunger have been as different as his? Would Joey have become, if filtering need through testosterone, just like Steve, minus the beauty? Would she seek, and conquer, and gather, and laugh, and leave? Would nothing be able to hold her down, pin her down, collect her? Would everyone around her bend to her will, as she would never again bend to anyone else's? Were these the only roles available for them, doormat or Don Juan?

Here she was, at last, on her journey of discovery, her adventure, the seventh son of a seventh son, her seven league boots eating the ground, never letting grass grow under her feet, off again with the sun to find another bed to warm for the night. Her sword strapped to her side, her clever guide and friend, loyal to the end of time, along with her on the journey. *It would be better if he were a talking cat*, Joey thought, *but I suppose fairy god reflection would do*. Even this, even the adventuring, was a role. Finding herself underneath was the real challenge, and Joey, in the silence of a deathly slow night at the restaurant, was discovering that. She missed Leela. Missed the wetness of her, the heat of her smile, the way she put on the extravagant, brazen approach, but revealed her tenderness underneath. Maybe she'd had better role models. She certainly seemed to be having fun, playing along. How had she avoided the U-Haul death of lesbian relationships? *Ouch*, Joey thought, *that's my scars showing*. Surely people were both gay and happy. Surely. Hadn't Steve flung an example in her face, many weeks back? Two women, dark and light, young and old, butch and femme, entwined, celebrating a decade. It did happen; if she found the right mirror, the reflection, no matter the variations, would prove true. So this wasn't a quest for a troll, or a giant, or a princess. Joey wasn't a clever tailor's apprentice, or a woodcutter, or a seventh son. It was a quest for a mirror, and she was just Joey.

Nine o'clock should have been busy, should have been the last quick rush for the last seating, but the main floor only had two tables full. Nobody was making any money tonight. Steve was long done with the side work and was wandering around tapping a spoon against his leg. Joey wished she still smoked. She could sneak out back in the parking lot for one. Or a dozen. The busboy was half asleep, propped up on his hand listening to a radio in the kitchen. The hostess was gone, along with three of the waiters. On any other night, Joey would have jumped at the chance to go play with Leela, rather than wander around making nothing, but they had picked this for their first night off. Brilliant, Joey thought, it had to be tonight. Maybe she could just stop by anyway, after her shift. Make some lame joke, and get herself invited in. No, that would send the wrong message. Not the booty call, that was true enough, and she did long for Leela's skin. Yet she didn't want to look like she was ignoring a boundary that had been set. How to vault over that, but not look like she was being too presumptuous? That was a skill that could only be learned through practice. Four days, well, five, of being with someone wasn't long enough to gauge their reaction for things like this. Particularly because they spent so much of their time together not speaking. So many conversations to have, and all of them would be great fun to get to, after they tore one another apart and destroyed the bed. Or the couch. Or the counter. Then somehow, it was the next morning, and they were going out, often with Steve and Kaori for company. Plenty of conversation, but not about certain things. At what point did it become time for the talking?

That was a relationship impulse. Joey recognized it and put it aside. Not yet. She'd never been here before, never had such an intoxication with a girl, never been so crazy about touching her, being near her. Why waste a moment of being awake and not be in touch with Leela's magnificent body? That was another thing Joey noticed. Leela was attractive, sure, anybody would say so. But after that first night, it was like the sun through a glass, focused and blinding. She got exponentially more gorgeous, until Joey couldn't look at her and think straight. Straight, funny, Joey thought. But did people always get better looking when you got to know them? It was a crime for certain people to wear clothing, that was for sure. Leela's heart-shaped ass, kept away from her adoring fans by rude denim, that was a tragedy.

The door to the restaurant opened. Steve perked up, like a dog at a familiar footstep, hearing the call of tips, then slumped back down. It wasn't a customer. It was Leela. Joey momentarily froze, wondering if her thinking had been loud enough to summon Leela. Then she saw what Leela was wearing. The skirt was blue, printed with golden flowers and swirls, sequins along the edge catching the light. Leela had been striking in jeans. This was a revelation. The cotton hung from her hips in ways that should be illegal, or mandatory, Joey wasn't sure. Was she wearing makeup?

Joey watched her walk across the largely empty floor, her hips tossing the skirt insouciantly. That was it, nobody else should ever bother wearing a skirt again, Leela alone had that right. How she could communicate volumes with the turn of her thigh.

"Hi," Leela said, softly, smiling through the word.

"Hi." Joey knew she was mirroring that smile. "What brings you to our fair deserted restaurant?"

"I know we were going to take a night off. But I was having dinner with my parents, and we were finished, and we were nearby, so I thought I might just drop in and say hello. That's not against the rules, is it?" Leela asked, her smile asking for more than forgiveness.

"If it is, I officially renounce the rules." Joey put her hand over her heart and swore, fervently.

"I have a confession to make. I just wanted to show you that I do get dressed up, sometimes." Leela spun in a circle, flaring her skirt out. Joey caught a glimpse of the back of her knee, of the beautiful shape of her ass.

"Holy God. I mean, yes, yes you do."

"I thought you'd like it. Is there somewhere we can go?"

"Go?"

"Just for a few minutes. To talk. It looks dead in here, they could spare you?"

"Nobody will notice I'm gone. There's an old storeroom upstairs. We could talk."

Joey pulled Steve aside. "Cover for me. I'm going to be upstairs in the storeroom with Leela."

"I'll have to start taking lessons from you. How do you make them show up at work?"

Joey took Leela's hand and led her through the kitchen, up a narrow staircase made more treacherous by piled boxes and cans. It was a fire trap. The top of the stairway was lost in darkness. Joey led the way out of long familiarity. The upstairs storeroom was well known to the staff, and officially not in use, but used for overflow of dry goods, spare tables, broken chairs, piles of old decorations. It was also used for all manner of illicit adventures. The wait staff would sneak off to smoke joints when the shift was slow enough and anybody was holding; the hostess used it to get better acquainted with the night manager. It was Joey's first time up these stairs for this reason. It made her dizzy.

There was light from a single bulb set in an old plasterwork sconce. Joey felt around the corner for the switch and flipped it on.

"Here you go, a tour of the fabulous upstairs storeroom. There are broken chairs, here a table, and boxes and boxes of crap." She pulled Leela in.

"Lovely," Leela said, not looking at any of it.

"You certainly are," Joey said appreciatively. Her hands roamed Leela's skin, running down her arms, tracing the inside of her wrists.

"I thought you liked your girls girly, so I had to show you that I can be a girl."

"You're always a girl to me, no matter what you wear. Just show up. So, you wanted to talk?"

"Yes," Leela said, shaking her head from side to side.

"Mixed messages, whoa."

"Kiss me."

Joey pressed Leela back against the table, lifting her up and sitting her on the edge. The skirt rode up on her thighs.

"Want to know the best thing about skirts?" Leela whispered in Joey's ear, as Joey was kissing her neck.

"Mmm."

Leela took Joey's hand and guided it. "Easy access."

"My God."

"I thought about you during dinner. A lot."

Joey's fingers brushed Leela's underwear, coming away wet. "I can tell."

"I had to press my legs together, hoping I wouldn't leave

the chair wet when I stood up. All I could think about was surprising you and begging you to touch me." Leela gasped, and folded against her when Joey's fingers kept exploring.

"You never need to beg."

Leela whispered in her ear again. "I want to. This is my adventure. You make it okay to be this way with you, to want your touch so badly that I'd beg for it."

"Then beg for it," Joey said, her voice like steel, imitating Naomi's stern tone.

"Please, Joey, touch me. Please." Leela squirmed under her hand, needing attention. "Ask me again."

"Hmm?" Joey couldn't quite follow Leela's train of thought, as hers was already set on getting Leela's underwear off. Leela helped, by lifting her hips off the table and letting Joey's fingers hook in the elastic. This turned out to be both very helpful and very distracting, as Joey slid her hands down Leela's legs.

"How I liked to be fucked."

Joey, kneeling between Leela's open legs, looked up with an evil grin. "How do you like to be fucked, Leela?"

"Urgently."

Joey liked this answer. It was a new one, one of the many to be added to the mosaic. There were times for feasting, and there were times to grab and wolf and devour. Joey stood back up, kissing along the way, and slid her hand under the now compromised skirt. The cotton clung to her as she touched Leela.

"You're so wet. Can't leave you like this."

"I need you."

It seemed to have slipped out. Leela looked surprised that she said it, but the touch of Joey's fingers moved the moment along and it was forgotten. The table rocked on its unsteady foundation to the push of Joey's hand. Leela put her hands down on the table to brace herself and lifted her hips to Joey. The table tilted precariously. Joey, her fingers still inside Leela, knelt down and braced the table with her free hand. Leela saw what she was doing and slid forward, balancing on the edge, presenting herself to Joey. It was a small leap of choreography to follow one motion with another, and add her lips to the melee. Joey's tongue circled Leela's clit, her fingers curled inside and up, nearly meeting through the heat of flesh.

Leela came, hard, curling forward over Joey, gasping. Her teeth closed on Joey's shoulder. Her shoulders shook, her arms trembled. She moaned. "Joey."

"I've got you, baby."

"Just hang on."

It was a few moments of perfect silence before Leela sat back up, and Joey stood.

"I'm soaked," Leela said, trying to put her skirt back in order.

"I hope that's bragging," Joey said, standing up.

Leela stopped fixing her clothing and took a surprised Joey's face in her hands.

"It sure is." She kissed Joey tenderly. "I should let you get back to work."

"Why? Oh, right, I'm still at work."

They made their unsteady way down the back stairs and into the kitchen. Steve, with a dramatically calm face, sipped at his coffee and watched them. Joey took Leela to the back door. "You can go out the staff way. Heck, you're practically family."

Leela kissed her, lightly. "I would hope so." She smiled over her shoulder as she went out the screen door. Joey slumped back against the counter and sighed.

"So, you going over to Leela's after work?" Steve asked, and started laughing.

"Nah. We talked about it, and we thought we'd take a night off."

Joey eventually crawled home. Perhaps a night off was a good idea, but when she brought her fingers to her lips, she smiled in recollection.

Friday was a week to the day since her first night with Leela. Six of the intervening nights and portions of the day had been spent with her, getting progressively drunker on their sexual connection. Leela was unbelievable, astounding; a shy girl cutting loose, having her own adventure. It hadn't occurred to Joey until Leela said it that she was stepping outside her normal bounds with their affair, that she was also playing a game with new rules. She wondered what Leela was learning from their time together.

Chapter Twelve

Joey wanted to see Naomi. She missed her, but she wanted to talk to her more than have sex. She had to tell her about Leela. Not that she had to, technically, as Leela was more of an organic encounter, not through the online ad, but, to be honest with herself, Joey admitted that without the ad and meeting Naomi, she'd never have met Leela or gotten involved with her. Not involved, no, Joey mentally corrected, just hanging out with.

"No sex, this time. I think I can spare a few minutes for tea, if you like." Naomi tossed her the keys and Joey let herself in.

Her first thought, as she was hugging Naomi, was *She's lost weight*. Her second was *She's not wearing makeup*. She'd always, even at four in the afternoon on a Wednesday, worn full dramatic makeup. The polish on her nails was chipped with wear and work. Her hair was pulled back in a lazy ponytail. Her eyes and lips were naked. There were bags under her eyes.

"Hi, Joey. Sit. How have you been?"

"Good, Mistress." Joey took the cup of tea offered her.

"You can call me Naomi today."

"Yes, uh, Naomi. How's your mom?"

Naomi put the kettle back on the stove. "Dying. But not in too much pain along the way, and that's all we can ask for, right? That, and a private island in the Caribbean."

"I'm sorry."

"Don't be. This is how it goes." Naomi pushed a plate of cookies toward Joey. "Have a cookie and tell me about the last few weeks."

Joey took an oatmeal cookie. "I met someone, Mist—Naomi."

"Oh, the closeted woman again?" Naomi asked, pouring herself a cup of tea.

"No, somebody new. Not through the ad, either. In a class we took together years ago. That was the first of the three."

"You met three times?"

"Well, a few weeks ago at the restaurant, then I ran into her on the street, then she hung around with Steve and Kaori, and that's when I officially met her for the first time."

"She's three times as ready as you for this, then. So you hit it off?"

"Not at first, no. But when we met again we did. Or she did. Remember when you said be open to women flirting with me? It was like that. I stood still and there she was. It was the most perfect thing I've ever encountered, the whole night with her."

"Have there been other nights, Joey?"

"A few. Well, a lot," Joey admitted.

"I see."

"We, all of us, hang out. And have meals together. And go out after work. But I don't go home with Leela every time."

"I'm glad to see that you are feeling better." Naomi poured Joey more tea.

"Thanks. What?"

"You must be, if you are evolving past your rules. So your

time is over as an adventurer. Well, even Odysseus went home eventually."

"What are you talking about? I thought you wanted me to meet other people."

"Oh, Joey, I do. I didn't know you were ready to start dating so soon."

"Dating?"

"What you described to me, spending time together with your friends, for meals, for evenings, and going home together, that sounds a lot like dating."

Joey pushed away from the table, but didn't get up. Where was there to go? She felt like pacing, like running, really. "Dating? We never said anything like that."

"What did you say, Joey?"

"Not much, I guess. We just started. It seemed so natural. I mean, she did know about the online ad and me not dating. She asked Steve. So she did know that before we got together."

Naomi looked at Joey over her teacup. "She'd heard it, yes. But it sounds like you need to have a conversation with her. Have you told her about me?"

"No, but I did tell her about Joyce."

"So she does know you are with other people. But have you been with other people since you started?"

"Right. I guess not."

"So why haven't you told her about me?" Naomi asked, persistent.

"I guess I didn't want to screw things up." Joyce wasn't any kind of a threat, it was once and gone. "Psycho Barbie stopped by recently and asked me to go out with her, and I said no. Leela was with me. That made me look good. But telling her about you, that's different. We've been friends longer. You mean a lot to me, and that's different to hear about. I was afraid things would get complicated."

"Things are already complicated, sweetheart. Even if you are only sleeping with one person, things get complicated. You wanted to be ethical about your adventures, right? That means Leela should get the whole story and be able to make up her own mind. Or are you going to break off things with me and pursue a relationship with her, if she isn't happy about you and me?"

"Wait a minute, she never said anything like that. I wouldn't break it off with you. You've been so good to me. You taught me so much. I'm not ready to be told what to do in a relationship."

"Relationships aren't all like that, Joey."

"No? Well, I just shook Psycho Barbie's crazy from my sheets. I don't need to go and get more complicated. I don't want to stop seeing you."

Naomi put her teacup down. "Oh, there goes my beeper. I have to run. Can you let yourself out, Joey?"

Joey's mind was full of clouds as she wandered home. She and Leela weren't dating. They hadn't said any of the dating things. They'd started out going 160 in a 30 zone, none of the romantic hand-holding. Making love all night in front of the glow of a small fire... *Ah, shit*, Joey thought, *we're dating*. She hadn't been expecting that, for it to just sneak up on her like that. Leela was already around, already friends with her friends, was fun and beautiful and warm, of course they would spend time together. That didn't mean that they were dating. Okay, she had to admit, they maybe had crossed a line or two. The siren song had beguiled her for a moment. All she had to do was set Leela straight. Er, make sure Leela was clear about things. Joey didn't date, it was right in the disclaimer. After dating came the bloodletting, the demands, the disappointments, the slow drip-by-drip death. It was even worse if she got emotionally attached. She prayed that it wasn't already too late. Joey tried an experiment; she pictured Leela's face when she came. The immediate contraction of her heart was a bad sign. This sort of thing only got worse if you paid attention to it. It was like a ghost; if you refused it power, it wouldn't be able to harm, or so Joey desperately hoped.

Joey half ran up the stairs to the apartment. Joey sat down on the couch, absently petting the sleepy cat. There had to be a center for her to find. Leela and she were dating. There wasn't another way to look at it, no matter the angle that Joey sought. It had sneaked up on her. Did it always? Psycho Barbie, that dead-eyed vortex of evil, reared her grotesque head, waving the lessons she'd taught Joey. *If you care for a girl, if you fall for her, she'll own you. And you can never be sure how she will treat you, once she owns you.* The image was enough to make Joey stand and start to pace, make her skin shiver like a horse shuddering off flies. Make her long to run away and never get caught. Make her turn a hard eye on adventuring as a long-term choice.

The glimpse of that horizon made her sit down again. That was a choice from pain, not from desire. But the pain was real, and had the voting rights of being with her longer. That was the whole point of the adventure in the first place, freedom, experience, no more pain. Psycho Barbie wasn't long gone, and her hand was still in Joey's pocket. Did it make any sense to be thinking of getting involved again? *Sure,* Joey thought, *girls are mighty attractive, when they look at you all doe eyed and melty, at first.* But then, she knew, it started getting all Vampirella. It was like throwing herself head first off a bridge. The rush on the way down was intoxicating. Did that mean she was willing to risk it again?

Steve came tramping up the stairs, flicked the lights on, and saw her. "Hey. You look grim as death."

"Brooding," Joey said, as Steve moved the cat and sat down next to her.

"Oh good, everything is normal."

"I think I know what I want to do. It doesn't look like any fun." Joey stood up and started pacing.

"What do you want?"

"I want a Storm to my Kitty Pryde. I want a Columbia to my Magenta, but just for that scene, you know? A Gabrielle to my Xena, Cagney to my Lacey."

"A Willow to your Tara?"

"Or a Tara to my Willow. I'm good either way."

"I would think more a Yukio to your Storm. Or Callisto."

"Hopey to my Maggie."

"Right, like you're not Hopey."

"Fine. A Francine to my Katchoo. But not yet."

"Okay, that makes sense." Steve watched Joey's pacing slow to a halt. "Better?"

Joey heaved a ragged breath. "Yeah. Somewhat. Tell me something. Why don't you ever have these existential crises over boys?"

Steve patted the couch next to him, and Joey sat. "I do. I just don't pace as much as you do."

"But you want love."

"That's one of the things I want, sure."

"What if it doesn't come along?"

"I have plenty of love in my life. I have you. And there are always other flavors that drift through, seasoning the sauce, so to speak."

"I think we're like plague victims. We're scarred for life by our upbringing. Our bones are weakened by a steady diet of disapproval, until we swill poison like it was Kool-Aid and smack our lips."

Steve looked at her with approval. "You're not often this poetic without drinking."

"What if I never found you?" Joey asked, her chin trembling. "I never would have made it out of that place alive."

Steve threw his arm around her shoulders. "No more bottomless pit of sullen depression. The important thing is, you did find me, and we both made it out alive. And we will keep making it out alive. And dammit, we will be happy if we have to level the city to do it."

"That's a little extreme."

"Says the 'my heart is an impenetrable fortress, I shall never love again' guy."

"Do I really sound that bad?"

"Nah. Just a little kicked around. You'll even out."

"Yeah, I guess. I have to talk to Leela, but I have to have a conversation with Psycho Barbie first." Joey thought, there would be no freedom for her, unless she faced that Gorgon. Joey made the call and set up a meeting with Psycho Barbie for coffee.

The next day, at the start of her shift, Joey came out into the dining room and Psycho Barbie was standing by the POS stand, waiting for her. Bloody, unconscionable, holy hell, Joey thought, walking over. She was early. A whole day early. They'd arranged to meet for coffee, but Psycho Barbie had changed the rules. She knew she'd get the upper hand in the conversation that way, keep Joey annoyed and off guard. Joey hadn't formulated everything she wanted to say yet. Psycho Barbie was unctuous in her greeting.

"Joey, so good to see you. Can we talk?"

"That was the plan. For tomorrow." Joey motioned her into the empty front room. They stood at the bar and faced the cold fireplace. "But go ahead."

Psycho Barbie was looking her up and down. It was unnerving, like being a fly in front of a reptile. "You look good, Joey. I'm hearing all over about your new adventures."

"Don't believe everything you hear."

"I'm impressed."

"I'm glad."

"I should be commended for seeing that spark in you, before you became the fashion."

Joey shrugged to get rid of the weight she felt. "What was it that couldn't wait?"

"After you phoned, I got to thinking, and I have a proposition for you. You've been on my mind a lot lately. I've been missing the good times that we had. We were something, weren't we?"

"Something, yes."

"Well, I think we were. And before you bring it up, I did ask you to move out, but I think that is a blessing in disguise. We've both had time to grow, and change, and I think you've learned a lot from this. That phone call asking to meet me told me everything I needed to know. We can get back together now."

"I'm sorry?"

"I'm not advocating that you move back in. I think it would make sense to take it slow, date one another again. But we can be exclusive. And to show your commitment, of course, you would renew the lease."

Joey felt a dark bubbling in her lungs, a wet sort of coughing laugh gather in her throat. That's what this was about? It was the last month on the lease, how had she forgotten that? Psycho Barbie wanted her to renew it and presumably keep on paying her rent, to prove her commitment to their renewed dating.

"That's quite an offer."

Joey wanted to delay the rest of this conversation, or continue it at home with Steve and Kaori rooting for her just a few feet away. But this was something that had to be faced alone, in silence. Her friends could come along on the journey up to the gate, but she had to be the one who chose to go through. More time. She wanted more time, to prepare. Psycho Barbie seemed to sense the brick wall behind Joey's eyes. The look on her face was comical, puzzled, her eyebrows rising up and down, her eyes round. This wasn't the reaction she'd anticipated, Joey thought. She watched Psycho Barbie decide that she just needed to seduce a little, let Joey know what the right response was, and she'd get it. That had never failed. So Psycho Barbie leaned in and wrapped an arm around Joey's neck, laughing, golden and desired, sure of it.

"Well?" Psycho Barbie's resumed presumption of success was evident in her voice.

"I thought about what you said, about our years together, and I decided that I owe you an apology." Joey looked her in the eyes, noting that the crystal blue was dancing, light on water. Psycho Barbie's face softened, ready to accept her triumph. There was in her, at that moment, something of the beauty that had so slain Joey when they first met. But that softness was fleeting, that concern and warmth were tools. Back in the box they'd go, as soon as the immediate need for them was gone.

"That's wonderful."

"I have to apologize to you for being such a doormat. If I hadn't let you treat me the way you did, maybe you wouldn't have kept on doing it. Maybe you would have developed a sense of shame, or of virtue, but I can't be your conscience for you. I have enough of a hard time being my own." The ease of it astonished Joey. Once she decided to start talking, it fell naturally, without pain.

"What?" Psycho Barbie's tone dipped right into dangerous, the arm uncoiled from Joey's neck.

"I won't be renewing the lease. In fact, I told the landlord I moved out months ago. I won't be paying your rent anymore. You have until the end of the month to find your own place." Simple truth, assured, without attack, just as she'd wanted. Once spoken, Joey felt the weight of the world fall away from her shoulders, weight she wasn't used to being without. It stunned her. All this time, all she had to do was stop consenting and set the weight down. She'd picked up self-respect instead, and Psycho Barbie could no longer take anything from her.

Psycho Barbie shook her head incredulously. "You must be joking."

"Not a bit." It was said kindly. Joey felt the calmness, the wholeness, of being responsible to herself. *This is why I always felt unbalanced, this is what I was so terrified of, saying no?* There was power in it, power that filled Joey head to toe.

"You can't do this to me. You owe me. You told me you would take care of me." The anger was out now, along with the claws. Usually, the first hint of anger was enough to shut Joey down.

"You told me you'd be faithful. We were both wrong."

Psycho Barbie started laughing, that cynical little chuckle she used to emasculate. "Who put you up to this? Steve, right? You haven't got the backbone. You never finish what you start, and you never follow through on anything. Like school. You didn't want to finish, or me simply asking wouldn't have derailed you. You never fight for anything. You run away, like you ran away from home."

That got through Joey's armor, and hurt. Blood started to leak from a dozen emotional wounds, torn open ruthlessly. She was conflicted about leaving home, about her distant relationship with her family, about not finishing school. About leaving her first relationship, failing at it. It had kept her in limbo, not able to move on, not able to let the old apartment go. Not able to let Psycho Barbie go. Psycho Barbie had her off balance, again.

"Maybe you are right," Joey said. "I don't finish what I start. Time I learned that. I'm done with you. You are a narcissistic asshole who uses people, then throws them away. You had your chance with me; now it's over. I'm done carrying your barge. You got feet, walk." *There. Go through the pain,* Joey thought, *there is freedom on the other side.*

"You will regret this," Psycho Barbie said, furious.

"Maybe. But I'm feeling pretty good about it right now." Joey turned around. She felt like singing. "See you around." Joey walked away, her stride free.

Steve approached from the dining room where he'd been lurking, his hands clasped in front of his chest. "Tell me what I think just happened just happened."

"Oh, that? I told Psycho Barbie to take a flying leap."

"What got into you?"

"She ambushed me a day early. I started thinking about love, and looked at the examples in my life. I finally came to the idea that anybody who doesn't treat me as well as my friends do doesn't have the right to be in my life."

"I've been saying that for how long?"

"I know. But until I came to it myself, nobody could tell me anything. So thanks. For sticking around even when it looked like I wasn't hearing you. It finally sank in."

❖

Joey finally picked up the phone the next afternoon and called. Leela sounded cheerful. "You coming over tonight, or am I meeting you out?"

"Can I come over now?" Joey asked.

She could hear the purr in Leela's voice, the assumption of afternoon delight. "Sounds good to me. Come on over."

The walk was too quick for Joey's taste, just around the corner. She dragged her heels, wishing she could walk all the way up Allen to Elmwood, then down Virginia to College and go the back way, but there wasn't time. Leela knew exactly where she lived, and knew how long it would take to get from Steve's apartment to hers. Joey rehearsed what she was thinking, trying to find the right thing to say. *Leela, I'm not looking for someone to date, not a romantic partner, not a lover.*

I'm good with affection, Joey thought, *but not the burning, drowning loss of self that Psycho Barbie was to me. Love screws everything up*, Joey thought. *Keep Psycho Barbie firmly in mind. The last time you gave in to this feeling, it ate your life.* She'd only just carved out the malignancy. It was too soon to open herself up for something unknown to take root. Not yet, no matter the blandishments. She just wasn't ready.

She rang the bell, and Leela came down happily to let her in. Joey's serious mien gave her pause, and she seemed to hesitate on reaching for a kiss. Joey took advantage of the hesitation and kissed her on the cheek. They walked up the stairs in silence.

Leela sat down on the couch, watching Joey very carefully. She was sensitive to the small signals of rejection, Joey noted, her face falling, her eyes shading. Leela knew something was up. It was always a surprise, the first time that lust and wetness and warmth morphed into something else and you had to learn the lineaments of anger, or of distance, on your lover's face.

Leela was having just such an educational experience, Joey could see it. She wondered what she looked like, if her brows were too far drawn down, meeting in an angry ridge over her nose, making her look like an evil Slavic ghost.

Leela was meeting the stranger in Joey. Joey could read the effect of her presence in Leela's transformation, from loving and playful to reserved. It settled over her like dust and hardened to armor in a few simple gestures—sitting back against the couch, crossing her legs, linking her hands in her lap. Leela was a different person, one in complete control of herself, not giving anything to Joey. It was that moment that Joey recognized how much Leela gave to her in all their encounters, the warmth, the connection, the attention. The removal of it was chilling.

"I suspect you are not here for a quick roll in the hay, so why don't you start talking?"

This is what Leela will be like in a fight, Joey thought. Controlled. Calm, rational. Just the thing to make Joey lose her composure, to be increasingly irrational and loud. It was, for Joey, the whip of silence and reason from her upbringing that had so driven her to an emotionally abusive person like Psycho Barbie. Their arguments had been spectacular, theatrical, and always ended the same way—with Joey's complete capitulation, no matter the subject. The very fire and drama that provided a thrill to Joey, that sounded like love to her, also made her terrified and brought her to heel. Psycho Barbie could yell, louder and longer, and so won every argument. This Joey knew about herself, even as she despised it. What would fighting with Leela be like?

There was such a feeling of approval from her at other times that the withdrawal felt like a slap. Joey resented it, though she knew she'd caused it entirely and was to blame for its continuance. She wanted that warmth and approval back, but feared the urge as a flaw within herself. It made her harsher, as she geared up for the battle.

Joey started to pace. "You remember the night I first came home with you?"

"I'll remember it until I die," Leela said calmly.

"Yeah." This wasn't going the way Joey wanted, not at all. Leela was able to acknowledge her affection for Joey quite calmly, despite Joey acting like a strutting prick right in front of her. Joey admired her courage even as she flailed against its expression.

"You talked to Steve about the online ad, right?"

"Right," Leela said, letting her find her own way through the maze.

"So you know I don't date, right?" Joey abruptly stopped and faced Leela.

"That's what I heard, yes." There her tone got a bit brittle; it was gratifying to Joey to see a hint of annoyance.

"Okay. But you and me, we've been spending a lot of time together recently. And some of it has been pretty datelike." Joey started pacing again.

"I can see that, yes."

"I just wanted to be clear. I'm not looking for someone to date."

"So I gather."

"There's more."

Leela looked at her, steadily, making Joey more nervous. Why was this hard?

"I met a woman though the ad, Naomi. Before I met you. She and I have been, well, not seeing one another, but sleeping together. For a while now."

"I see." Leela's eyes glanced down, then back at Joey. There was no heat in the Madeira.

"Not since we, you and I, got together. She's got some major stuff going on. But she'll be free soon. And I want to be able to keep seeing her."

"Well, I rather expected that."

This stopped Joey dead in her tracks. "You did?"

"Of course I did, Joey. Your reputation was clear. We're together constantly, we make love like it's going out of style, but we're friends. I get the message."

"You do?"

"You're a desperado, out riding fences. You're a freelance in the mercenary wars of love. I get it. You are involved with other people. Does this mean you won't be involved with me?"

"No, I mean, I should sit down." Joey did so, and looked at Leela. She was being understanding. This was what Joey had wanted, wasn't it? Why was Leela's understanding making her more agitated? It would be fine to keep on seeing Naomi, and have Leela to come to. Yet when she pictured that, a knot formed in Joey's stomach. She didn't want to come to Leela, fresh from Naomi's bed. It didn't seem right. It seemed profoundly wrong. "This isn't coming out right. Do you know why I'm doing this in the first place?"

"Psycho Barbie. Steve told me."

"Did he? Let me detail it a little for you. I was a dumb kid fresh from a farming town, never been with anyone before, when I met her. I was stupid with hunger. She wanted me. Nobody had ever wanted me before. I thought I was supposed to do everything she asked, no matter what it was, to prove my love and loyalty, a notion she played upon if not originated. We were together for close to four years. I gave up everything, and she took more. I still have nothing but scars and ashes, and a pile of bills that I still pay. My life just isn't the same. She broke my heart." This speech was delivered without additional embroidery, flat as a stone.

Leela looked away. "You seem like you're doing all right to me."

Joey wanted, right then almost more than anything, to have Leela look at her again. "It's an act."

"You are an accomplished actor." This was cold, clipped. It hit home.

"I'm not ready to give up seeing Naomi, is what this is," Joey said, feeling more foolish by the moment.

"I don't recall asking you to," Leela said, her voice sharpening. "I don't want your freedom."

"I want yours," Joey said, before she could think about it. Leela gasped.

"That's the problem. I've enjoyed every minute I've spent with you. Every single one. I look forward to seeing you again. My friends adore you."

"Why does that sound ominous, when it should make me feel fantastic?" Leela held her hand to her chest.

"Why are you in this, Leela? What do you expect from me?" It was Joey's plan to try to get the conversation under control, to sound like Naomi. It didn't work.

"Why am I in this? Do you mean, why am I sleeping with you, and spending time with you and all your friends? Why am I being nice to you? Are you that dense? I can be a raving bitch if that gets through to you. It certainly has in the past. It will be an effort, but I can try."

"Leela."

"Don't bloody well say my name like we're in bed. We're not in bed. We're on my couch and we are having a fight, thank you very much, so you don't get to say my name like that."

"Okay."

"I got into this because I like you. I've liked you since I saw you in class. You seemed sweet, and handsome, and clever. Then I find out that you are free, and having your cake and eating me, too, well, why not? I thought I could be clever, be a free spirit, too, and have an adventure of my own. With you. And you know, it was wonderful, to be that person, the one who picked you up, who took you home, who wanted you so badly she couldn't see straight."

"Leela."

"So why are you in this, Joey? What do you want?"

"I wanted experience."

"So, now you have your experience, you're telling me that you don't want any more? There's more to me than my body."

"I know."

"Or maybe the body isn't good enough for you?"

It had worked. She'd gotten Leela angry enough to be irrational. It settled in Joey's stomach like a pit. She felt like crawling away to die. Leela's pain was too much for her. She took Leela's head in her hands and kissed her, until Leela softened and reached for her.

"Stop. Just stop. You know that your body is magnificent, and I'm addicted to it."

"Are you in love with her?"

"Not romantically. But in a way."

"I see."

"She's been good to me. I don't want to be ungrateful."

"I see."

"I'm not ready for more. But when I'm with you I start to want it."

"So to avoid wanting something, you are going to avoid me?"

"Something like that, yes." It didn't sound any better out loud, and Joey felt ridiculous. Worse, Leela's beautiful eyes were glassy, about to spill over into tears.

"What if I already really care about you, and want to keep on seeing you?"

"With me seeing other people?"

"If that has to be the way."

"It doesn't feel right."

"What if it were more than caring?"

Joey knelt down and took Leela's hands. "I'm sorry. I can't do big emotion. Not yet."

Leela leaned her forehead against Joey's, her tears starting. "I hate it."

"I know."

"No, you don't. I hate that you're a fucking teenage boy and I should know better, no matter how cute or clever you are. I hate that you are so twisted up that you have to break up with me so you don't start seeing me."

Joey pushed away and stood up again. "I'll see you around, okay?"

"I won't hold my breath."

CHAPTER THIRTEEN

Naomi called her, at last. Her mother had passed away, the previous Saturday. She sounded sad but calm, resigned.

"It was time for it. It is never easy, but it was time. What about you, Joey? How have you been?"

"Fine, Mistress." What was there to say about her life, that even compared to what Naomi had been through in the past few weeks?

"Good. I'd like us to get together soon, if that works for you. I've been missing our time together, and I certainly could use a distraction."

"I'd like that, Mistress."

"Time for some boundary pushing. My partner, Vic, would like permission to call you. Would that be all right?"

"Yes, Mistress." *What in the world*, Joey thought.

"Good. I'll give her your number. You know, of course, that you have the full right of refusal for anything you don't want to do."

"Yes, Mistress." It felt good to have someone else be in charge again.

"Good. Expect her call tomorrow."

Joey now had something to look forward to, and it did

help. She clung to the distraction. When the phone rang the following afternoon, she beat Steve to it and glared murder at him till he backed off. This wasn't going to be like any of her other exploratory phone calls.

"Joey?" Vic's voice was deep and rough, as Joey had imagined it, grained like hardwood. Joey felt a shiver run up her spine. This was the real deal, a butch so powerful she could make a woman come just by looking at her. Joey felt very much like a puppy confronting the big dog.

"Yes. Vic, right? Naomi said you would call."

"I have a proposition for you. I know that you've been playing with Naomi and have taken a few steps into some more elaborate scenes. You know that Naomi's mother passed recently. Naomi's been having a rough time of it. She looked after her mom for years. She has a lot of emotion built up and needs to release it, needs to be taken out of herself, out of her head, and just feel. I think that together, we can do that for her. What do you say?"

"Sure. I mean, yes, of course I'd like to help."

"Great. Come on over to Naomi's on Friday, normal time. I'll leave the keys in the box. Naomi will be upstairs in the dungeon."

"The attic?"

"Right. You are a literalist, Naomi mentioned that. Yes, the attic. Here's what I'm thinking. You bring an overnight bag."

Joey agreed. She had learned how to pack an overnight bag by now. Toys, harness, condoms. "Got it."

"Good. Naomi, as you know, is good at being in charge, at running a scene. She's so much in charge in her daily life, and was so responsible for all her mom's care, that she hasn't been out of that power dynamic in weeks. Plus, she's grieving, but can't reach the emotion to release it. She needs to be taken out of herself. I know her limits and know what she needs. I'll take her to the edge, before you come in. Then you follow my lead, and we can make her very happy."

"Of course," Joey said, trying to sound both nonchalant and ready.

"Good. Nothing fancy, just straightforward topping. I'll have her tied up in a whipping posture already. Put your harness on, under your jeans, and meet me upstairs."

Joey hung up the phone. She had her distraction now.

When she fished the keys out of the mailbox at Naomi's, she noticed that the nameplate was missing from the lower bell. *How quickly the mundane details change and adjust when the important things are gone*, Joey thought. Joey took the steps two at a time. The kitchen door was open. In the kitchen was a butch woman in her late forties or early fifties, short, dark hair threaded with gray, stocky build, broad shoulders, square. Her face was solid, lined, serious, firm. Her eyes, pale blue under dark brows, spoke of knowledge and self-confidence. This was a woman who would back down from nothing. She gave off such an aura of power that Joey felt the shiver again. This was the Big Dog. The hand she held out to Joey was blunt fingered, square, powerful, scarred. Joey took it and tried not to give a limp handshake in return. It was like looking into a distortion mirror that showed the future. In thirty years, if she was lucky, she might have a presence like Vic's. She might be the biggest dog. She might be able to make a woman come just by looking at her. The role model she'd been looking for was right here, shaking her hand.

"Hi, Joey." In person, Vic's voice was even deeper.

"Hi, Vic." Joey was entirely at a loss for words. Naomi

she could chat with, even question. Vic intimidated her into speechlessness.

The stairs to the attic were in the hallway between the dining room and the bedroom. Joey climbed them gingerly, afraid to make any untoward squeaks. The door was open at the top of the stairs. The attic was a single long room, hung with black cloth from the exposed rafters on down. The floor was padded with several rugs. From the rafters hung lengths of chain, a wooden bar attached by smaller link chains, complete with eyehooks, a structure of rough wooden beams mounted against the far wall allowed for various chaining positions. Naomi knelt, arms above her head, restrained by black leather cuffs clipped to a chain. She'd been recently whipped. A blindfold covered half her head, blocking her ears as well. Sensory deprivation, Joey thought.

There was a wall with various hooks, rings and chains, some with attached manacles, some empty. Next to the wall of chains was what looked like a well-ordered workshop, with whips of various kinds hanging.

"Is she ready?" Joey whispered, even though Naomi was blind and deaf at the moment.

Vic ran her fingertips across Naomi's shoulders. Joey shivered. "She's like a block of stone. She is very proud of her endurance. She tried to resist me. But I know what she can endure, how far within herself she can retreat and keep that part safe from what happens out here. That's the usual starting point. She can see, then, that she's proven something to me, that I respect her strength. Now we will start to tear her walls down with tenderness."

"Yes, Vic."

"Take your shirt off," Vic said calmly.

Joey peeled her T-shirt off and left the sports bra on. Vic didn't seem to object.

Vic unbuckled Naomi from the wall. Joey hurried to Naomi's other side and helped catch her when she sagged forward into Vic's arms. Vic removed the blindfold. Naomi's eyes were half closed, tears gathered at the sides. Tenderly, Vic smoothed back Naomi's hair. Naomi started to sob, collapsed in Vic's arms. She howled, clawed at the floor, wept, covered Vic in tears. It was a primal release. The emotions she had not previously been able to access were now released in a flood of tears, rending and clawing. Joey stood back and watched.

The rage blew down to grief, and as soon as Joey recognized the change, Vic motioned to her. "Help me."

They took Naomi by the arms and helped her down to the second floor and into the bedroom. There they lay Naomi on her back as the tears came down.

"We opened the door. Now we bring her back."

It was a song. A dark, funereal song, a requiem, but the melody ran like a river under the moon, polished black and reflecting light. The darkness gave contrast needed to see, to mirror. Vic started the caretaking, vanishing and coming back with a basin of warm water and a few soft cloths. She took one and started to clean Naomi's face, with a tenderness and delicacy Joey wouldn't have credited this battle-scarred warrior as owning, let alone showing in front of a young pup like her. She never told Joey what to do, simply set the example, in silence, and did what was right and what she expected, and Joey caught on quickly. In a moment she was cleaning Naomi's feet, while Vic took care of her neck and shoulders. Tears mixed with the water from their ablutions.

Joey knew that it took time for Naomi to find her way back from even a simple scene, so this was going to be a journey back through the dark with her eyes sewn shut, motherless daughter, needing both the strong hands now protecting her and the strong hearts anchoring her back to her body, her life.

In choosing the way, Vic had shown her knowledge of decades. What she gave was what Naomi needed, not what Vic wanted to enact upon her, Joey saw. When Naomi started to open her eyes and focus, she looked at Vic. Joey was holding her legs, moving up from her feet.

Once Naomi was present, Vic started kissing her. The first kiss looked to Joey like a greeting, a welcome back. It was hard to spot the exact moment when that changed, who tossed the spark on the tinder, but it caught and ushered in a conflagration. Joey wondered if she should put the cloth down and leave, the kiss was that intimate. Yet Naomi knew she was there, and Vic didn't give any signal to get gone, so Joey stayed and got her education in one of the faces of grief.

Death passed by, life got sweeter. It was grisly, if Joey thought too much about it, the reason for this upwelling of desire, the filling of absence. Naomi kept kissing Vic but took Joey's hand, and she started to get it. Not grisly; it was Life reasserting itself through the channels available, excess and recovery being part of that path. To scorn the path was to scorn the gift, the life returning to Naomi. If she walked away now, Joey knew, she'd regret it for the rest of her life. This was the distilled form of the lesson she needed to learn, how to live beyond the pale, beyond the town limits of Eden, how to meet another lost soul and make a trail through the dark using only their own blood and the stars as guide. Find me and bring me home, though you and I and home do not exist. Create the world anew, in a fashion that fit. There was no book to go to learn this lesson that Joey had ever read, nothing that would even mention it, let alone lovingly.

Joey let Naomi's hand anchor her, and Vic's example provide a guide. She moved up Naomi's body, kissing as she went. The circle flowed. Vic kissed Naomi's lips, Joey kissed her neck. Vic moved to Naomi's left breast, Joey to her right.

Together, they brought her up, started her hips moving, her feet slipping against the sheets, the sheets falling away. Joey stayed a half step behind Vic, watching her like a hawk, taking the harmonious line to echo hers. The big dog and the puppy, in tandem, cast the net.

Vic glanced at her, ceding place, indicating with a single flick of her steel eyes where she was going. Joey took the counterpoint, hoping she wasn't just gilding the lily, providing useless ornamentation. She wanted to be able to focus on Naomi, she wanted to watch Vic. She saw the strength of Vic's hands when they took Naomi's wet thighs and pushed them, roughly, apart. After the warmth and build of the caresses until then, this was a surprise to Joey, who thought the entire scene would be similarly tender. Yet Naomi responded exponentially to the firmness of the touch, showing all the signs of desire that Joey had come to know and several more, clearly ready to fling herself into abandon under Vic's firmest touch. She saw Vic's head, gray hair clipped like a suburban lawn, between Naomi's thighs. Joey wished she could know what Vic was doing, but to read the efficacy from Naomi's reaction was enlightening. If she'd ever wanted to know if Naomi ever came undone, here was the proof. She writhed like a schoolgirl under Vic's ministrations.

Vic looked up at Joey as she pushed herself up on her powerful arms.

"Come here."

Joey did, joining Vic. Vic buffeted Joey on the shoulder, nearly knocking Joey off her feet. "Fuck her."

Joey reached for the zipper on her jeans. "Leave them on. Just pull your cock out."

The jeans needed to be opened enough to pull out the toy, to settle the harness on her broad hips, and so they slipped down Joey's ass, but they stayed as she climbed between Naomi's thighs. She recognized quickly why Vic told her, ordered her, to keep her jeans on. Naomi reared up and grabbed at her, hands reaching for purchase and finding the denim a handhold. She clung to it, and to Joey's hips, as Joey topped her for the first time. Joey knew that Vic was operating largely in silence, not asking Naomi's desires or preferences, taking her where she needed to go. Joey would have liked to ask her how she wanted to be fucked, but there are other ways of asking. She listened to Naomi's body, the embrace of her thighs and the clutch of her hands, and fucked her, hard and fast, fucked her to remind her that she was alive, she was a body as well as a profound ache, that there were things for which it was worth keeping the flesh.

She pounded at Naomi's hips, pushed from her feet and back from her shoulders, put every swing and twist and imaginative flair in that she could. Her toes curled against the bed to gather traction. Naomi's hands pulled so hard on her jeans that they fell halfway down her thighs, but Joey didn't care. She was in the moment, focused on Naomi, bringing her higher than she'd ever been able to. In that space, Joey got a glimpse of what her own power would be like, in the coming years. Naomi started to shake seismically, cascading the lushness of her flesh. When Vic took over and rode Naomi, when Joey offered her slick cock to Naomi's mouth to suck, she felt her powerful breath on the back of her neck.

The sheets clung to Naomi's back, stippled with sweat.

She lay, half on her side, kissing Joey. Naomi turned and kissed Vic, who lay on her other side. She was moving slowly, she was soaked and pounded and torn to pieces, but she was present. Joey met Vic's eyes across Naomi's back. There was a hint of approval there that seemed sweeter than any words ever said to Joey.

Naomi's bed was huge, but Joey felt the scene evaporate

as it always did, felt the press of the world come back. The next moment had to be thought about, sleep, skinning off or pulling back on her soaked jeans, the harness she was still wearing, the cock pointed up at the skylight, Naomi very naked and Vic half naked next to her in bed.

Joey started the choreography of getting up. Naomi was collapsed against Vic's chest, cradled there, passed out. Joey lifted her eyebrows, and Vic nodded and smiled.

It was thanks, and farewell. Joey pushed her cock back into her jeans, pulled the zipper up, and made her exit.

The bus ran at this hour, but Joey felt like walking. It took more than an hour to walk from Kenmore to Allentown, but the night was cool and clear and in its stillness as perfect as she'd ever seen Buffalo. Joey felt a sense of peace with the evening. She was relieved to be up and gone. It was different with Vic there, naturally, but it was also different with Naomi now. She had crossed some kind of a bridge. Maybe she hadn't impressed Naomi yet, but she did bring her to a place where she wasn't in control, and then she brought her back. It was intoxicating, it was educational, it was profound, but it was also silent.

Here Joey allowed herself a stab of longing, for Leela. She wanted the caressing, the intensity, of their afterplay, the emotion of it, the connection. Not to be wandering the streets, clean and empty and alone, though that was where her actions and her desire had brought her. Yet if she had been with Leela, she wouldn't have had this night with Vic and Naomi. She wouldn't have been there to, finally, give something to Naomi that she needed. The pride added a bounce to her step. Joey was feeling a sense of her own power. It was funny how natural it seemed, how it had almost always been there, waiting. No ghostly finger writing on the wall, no lighting and clouds parting and choirs of seraphim, just a rising like the tide, and there it was as if it had always been.

CHAPTER FOURTEEN

It was Wednesday before Joey heard from Naomi again. On the phone, she sounded brighter, more like herself, than Joey had heard in weeks. Perhaps her attentions with Vic had been helpful. Well, Joey admitted, more than perhaps, she had seen the results for herself. It was also the first thing Naomi, sensitive to form, mentioned.

"I wanted to thank you for the other night. You worked wonders, you and Vic. It was like a dream, two handsome butches all over me."

"Thank you, Mistress."

"You've become quite the lover, Joey."

"You taught me, Mistress."

"I had a good pupil. Gifted. That's all teachers dream of, really."

"Yes, Mistress."

"Enough about me. How did it go with the girl you were seeing? Did she understand when you talked, and is everything all right now?"

Joey put her hand to her head. "We talked. I broke it off with her."

"Oh? She didn't take it well?"

"No, she did, well, she didn't, but she was game to try."

"Then why did you break it off?"

Joey's body slumped. She lay down on the couch, still holding the phone. Everything was too heavy. "I didn't want to be wanting her the way I was."

"I see. Did it help?"

No, Joey thought, *it made it much worse.*

"In a way."

In the way that now Leela was at least free to pursue other options that might treat her better than Joey did. In the way that now Joey was free, and wasn't freedom just another word for... *What was that lyric*, Joey thought. *Something about freedom.* She couldn't recall.

"Did you let her know that your time together was valuable and pleasurable, and thank her for it?"

"She wasn't much keen on hearing anything like that."

"Was she angry?"

"Sad angry, I guess."

"It can't have been that bad, from what you've told me. No promises were made, no vows, no declarations. You had fun, you move on, both of you."

It wasn't like that, Joey thought, but she didn't know exactly what it had been like, so she let it go. All she knew was she'd hurt Leela to protect herself, or maybe to keep from hurting her worse in the future. "Yes, Mistress."

"Yes, well. I need a rest after last Friday, as you can well imagine. I called you for another reason. There is a fund-raiser at the UU Church on Elmwood. You know, world music, multiculti food, dancing, good cause, all that hippie crap. I took my mom every year, but this year she won't be going. I feel obligated to show. Everyone knew her and would take it hard if I didn't make an appearance. But frankly, I can't face the idea of going alone. Would you be my escort?"

"When is it, Mistress?"

"Friday."

"Shall I meet you at home first, or meet you there?"

"Meet me at home, sweet Joey. You can drive, right?"

"I can. I don't get much practice."

"We'll take my car. I hate driving. It is always a treat for me when I can lasso someone else into the chore."

Joey spent days pondering what to wear, without the effervescing joy she once had while choosing costume to visit Naomi. She should be happy, Joey told herself. This was one of her dreams. She was going to walk up Elmwood with Naomi, and people would know they were together. Together. In fact, as she'd been formally asked to be an escort. Wasn't this a date? This was the time to dress up, put on her best shirt, slick her hair down and wear a tie and a jacket. Not the time to be feeling like her insides were getting cut out.

The scene with Vic had been one thing, important, unique, inarguably something she needed to participate in and know. This was a date. And, Joey thought, miserable, if she was going to date, why wasn't she with Leela? It had been weeks now.

She hadn't seen Leela, nor called, nor strolled by, though she easily could. Joey had hoped, fiercely, that she would see Leela around the neighborhood, but was thwarted. Leela had vanished. Steve was better about it, but Kaori started to sulk, clearly missing Leela and missing the time they all spent together. Joey felt the sting of implied disapproval, and stopped hanging out as much. More and more of her time was spent alone, walking, hiding in her barrackslike room, silent but for the throaty meows of Bakka-neko when he wanted in.

In the silence Joey found herself annoyed, bored, then terrified. It was too much like the emptiness of her youth.

This time, she didn't charge right out and grab Steve, grab Kaori, go drinking, distract herself. She sat, still. She endured the emotion that washed over her. She went through, point by point, her years with Psycho Barbie, from their initial meeting, to Psycho Barbie demanding that she drop out of school and work full time, to the moment when Psycho Barbie kicked her out of her own apartment. The years looked different to her now. She could see all the red flags, the moments when, now, she would run screaming into the night rather than let someone else treat her this way. Joey saw clearly the moments when her compliance, or her choices, built and sustained the monster that Psycho Barbie became. It wasn't a pleasant realization.

Joey did get dressed up for the fund-raiser, putting on her best white shirt, crisp and pure as armor, a black tie and suit. It had been a find, at AmVets, a suit roughly in her size, for less than ten dollars. The lapels were a little too deep for the decade, the material had too much of a shine, but it was black, it was a suit, and it was hers. Steve helped her take it in and let it out, tailor it to her. It worked. When she showed up at Naomi's door, Naomi was speechless. For a moment.

"You look so handsome, Joey. Older. I almost didn't recognize you."

"Thank you, Mistress."

"Just Naomi tonight. We're going out in public, no need to be explaining to all the good social justice folks about the Mistress thing. The handsome boi half my age is enough of an eye raiser."

"Yes, uh, Naomi. You look wonderful, too."

She did, clad in rust and scarlet, a shawl across her shoulders, the jewelry and makeup back to their dramatic level. It was an act, Joey realized with a hollow knock to her chest. Naomi was putting on a scene for the people who had known and loved her mom, taking up the mantle and responsibility of representing her in the world. Of course this was important. It wasn't likely to be enjoyable, but it was important.

When they got to the church hall, Joey could see that Naomi wasn't exaggerating when she said her mom had known everyone. Two out of every three people they passed, Naomi's hand on Joey's arm, stopped them to express condolences and remember her mother. Naomi bore this all with a weary grace and her usual humor, sounding forced to the ignored Joey on her arm. *I'm a prop tonight*, Joey thought, and acted accordingly, standing up straight, looking alert, fetching Naomi drinks, and largely left to the background. She chose a spot on the steps behind Naomi's chair and leaned on the rail, watching people come and go. Some of them she recognized. Elmwood was part of Allentown, and she paid attention to her neighborhood.

The thought occurred to her idly, then accelerated. Neighborhood people were here. Leela might be here. It made Joey stop leaning, stand up very straight. Was this the sort of event Leela would come to? It seemed likely, the venue, the purpose, the execution, the causes. Joey, led on by that hope, started to pray for it, *Please, let Leela show up*. Then, picturing it, she started to pray for the exact opposite, pray that Leela not set foot anywhere near the Unitarian Church tonight. She wanted to see Leela, she didn't want Leela to see her, and she particularly didn't want Leela to see Naomi.

All evening Joey had managed not to say anything about Leela, not about missing her, not about the ache, the guilt, of breaking it off. Nor, indeed, would the blinding hope, the roller-coaster tip into gravity knocking her stomach into her pancreas be discussed. The evening was almost over, the charity function closing down, the musicians drifting off one by one as the tables were rolled back and the chairs stacked. People drifted from the dance floor to the coat rack. Joey lowered her guard with a sigh. It was like singing a eulogy all night, and knowing no one else could hear it. Except Joey had the feeling that Naomi knew she was singing.

"Almost over, Joey. Can you stand a few more minutes?"

"Yes," Joey said, watching the crowd leave.

Naomi was displeased with her company, she could tell. She wasn't clever, or witty, or engaged. She wasn't present. At least she was present physically, Joey thought. Beyond that was asking too much. They had made it through the night. It was over. Then she looked to the door.

It was all over Leela's face, she hadn't been expecting to see Joey here. Joey, still on the steps in her suit. She couldn't look away. It was that terrible, sere, blasted look of intense sadness, that Joey knew was the reflection of longing, of naked desire.

"Joey, would you get my coat?" Naomi asked, standing up and looking at Joey. Joey was staring at the front door.

"That's her, isn't it?" Naomi asked, seeing Leela react to Joey, and Joey react to Leela. The length of the room was still between them.

"Yeah." Joey could see how Leela, surprised, open, was taking in the sight not only of her, dressed for a date, but also Naomi, who was speaking very intimately to her.

"You haven't seen her since you talked?"

"I haven't spoken with her, since," Joey said, looking away from Leela.

Leela continued to look at Joey's turned head, a question on her face. When Joey didn't look up, she turned away.

Naomi watched Joey. "She kisses you every time she looks at you."

"She does?" Joey asked, looking after Leela. Leela was pushing back through the crowd toward the doors. In a moment, she was gone from the church.

"And you kiss her right back," Naomi said.

"Do I?"

"You can't be this sanguine. The girl is clearly in love with you."

Joey looked at the tips of her shoes. "We never said anything like that."

"It's time for us to talk."

"Okay."

"I'm serious, Joey. I think we're at an end."

"What? You're just punishing me now. I told you, I stopped seeing her."

"I'm not punishing you, sweetheart. I'm setting you free. Deep down, you're not poly. You admitted that to me. It is not the libertine that attracts you, but the chaste, romantic image of the knight. You'll really be at your best when you can give your whole heart to a woman who loves you back, just as hard. That's fine. You have a beautiful young woman give you looks of melting passion, just to see you pass by. That's fine, too. But these things mean I have to let you go."

"I thought I was doing so well. I thought you were proud of me." There were tears in Joey's eyes, crowding onto her cheeks. Leela had walked away. She couldn't bear this loss, too. Somebody had to want her.

"Of course I'm proud of you, darling. That's why I'm letting you go. She's the one you need to be learning from now."

"You know what, I've had my fill of learning for now. I think I'm all done." Joey handed the keys to Naomi. The buoyancy that anger lent her was fragile and wouldn't stand more speech.

"You are a cheeky little bastard, aren't you? Planning a bratty exit because you don't like what you're hearing?" Naomi looked at her with eyes of thunder. "Stay where you are and listen to me."

Joey nodded, mute.

"I am going to add some information to the mix, so we are both clear. You and I are done. No more scenes, no more adventures, got it?"

Joey nodded.

"Good. You also need to know that I am not punishing you. I've enjoyed, treasured, our time together. You were a gift to me, a very unexpected gift, and you helped me through a very rough time in my life." This was said with more tenderness.

"Thank you," Joey said, violating the rules.

"I promised you that I would push your boundaries and I am going to. This is my last command to you. Get your ass back to school."

"Mistress?"

Naomi placed an envelope into Joey's hand. "I paid your tuition for next semester. You start classes in three weeks."

Joey looked at the envelope, incredulous. "Naomi, I can't—"

"You will also never say those words to me again. You are a remarkable, clever, handsome girl that I have come to love very dearly. I'm your friend. You will let me do this."

Joey hugged Naomi, who returned it.

"It also wouldn't kill you to tell Psycho Barbie off."

"Already done."

"There you go, I knew there was hope for you."

Joey was left alone, marching up Elmwood, back toward Allentown. Her stride was forceful, keeping her always in motion, always avoiding the trap of sitting still, determined to ride this one out. It was a roller coaster of a night. She missed Naomi already, she was grateful to be free, she was overwhelmed with the gift. Too many things. When she set her mind to desire, to see what she wanted, it kept going back to things she couldn't have. Elmwood met Allen Street and she took the right, heading back toward Days Park. She hesitated near the turn-off for Leela's apartment. It was only a few steps out of her way, she could go and knock on that door and beg forgiveness.

Forgiveness for what, Joey thought, angry again. What had she done? She turned away from the path to Leela's, and kept on Allen. She passed right by Nietzsche's, the bar, and was half determined to go home, but Steve and Kaori were there, and even they were down on her for making it no longer possible for Leela to hang out. Leela again, every direction she turned. Joey turned into the bar.

Inside it was a Mardi Gras parade come to rest, weird wooden sculptures made from driftwood and paint hanging from the ceiling, walls made up of graffiti and handmade posters for musical events, open mike night, visiting singers. A tall, lanky, wild creature of a poet was behind the bar, pouring drinks, a red-haired poet librarian was in the far back on the stage, rocking the mike, Kali Yuga, Kali Yuga, to a tight knot of people at small tables on the floor. It was the neighborhood arts bar. Everyone was a musician, or writer, or performer, or sculptor. Everyone treated Nietzsche's like their living room, and spoke with distaste of the tourists who would congregate there on certain nights. Ani DiFranco had gotten her start there, playing on open mike nights. The crowd was neighborhood, and so mixed gay and straight. Joey was glanced at as she came in, tossed two dollars cover to the man with the ponytail working the door, then largely ignored. A woman in a suit wasn't enough to draw comment.

Joey sat down on a bar stool, her back to the window, at the far end. The open mike poetry was removed by a magnitude of space, so she was left caressing the highly polished wood of the bar and trying to hide. She loosened her tie. Most of the crowd was in the back by the stage, a few were on the face of the bar, and nobody near her. Except, Joey noticed, for a very quiet, brown-haired girl in the corner on a slightly lower mismatched stool. Joey checked her out while waiting for the lanky poet behind the bar to cast a lazy, charming smile her way and saunter over.

The girl was around her age, maybe twenty-four, had straight brown hair of a medium chestnut shade that she wore long and parted in the center. She seemed quite average, even plain, until she looked up at Joey and smiled. Two things were striking about her: the warmth of her brown eyes, and the confident greeting in her smile. This young woman knew who she was and seemed to genuinely enjoy being cast up by fate on the same bar shore with Joey. At least, so her smile intimated.

"You here for the open mike?" she asked.

Joey shook her head. "Just passing by. I live around the corner."

"Me, too. Over on Mariner. You?"

"Days Park."

"Hey, neighbor."

"Hey. You here for the open mike?"

The girl smiled again, that warm and welcoming smile. "Yes. Had to hear Celia do the Kali Yuga, it's my favorite. But I read some, too."

"That's cool. You're a writer?"

"I wouldn't go that far. I write some. Among many other arts my parents insisted on." The girl held out her hand. "I'm Goblin."

"Joey."

"Heh."

"What's funny?"

"My pop's name is Joe."

"I hope that's a good association."

The lanky poet slunk and strolled over, and leaned on the bar. "What can I get you? You good, Goblin?"

"Another ginger ale would be great. What about you, Joey?"

"Whisky."

The poet smiled, tilted her head at Goblin, and walked away, languorous.

"Goblin is an unusual name, if you don't mind my saying."

"I don't mind a bit. It's a nickname. The law thinks my name is something else again, but since even my parents have called me this as long as I can remember, this is my name."

"I get it. Joey's a nickname, too. What is it with dykes and nicknames?" She saw something flicker across Goblin's face, not distaste, but some recognition.

"I'm sorry, I shouldn't presume," Joey said.

"You wouldn't be far off, depending on the day of the week. No, I was just thinking about a conversation I had with a friend about the same thing. She said exactly what you did."

"She a dyke?"

"The king of them."

"Then there you go." Joey wasn't sure what she'd just proven, but the barpoet was back with her whisky. She took the tumbler and tossed off a large swallow.

"What's her name?" Goblin asked.

"The reason I'm drinking? Take your pick."

"Ouch. Well, if she broke your heart, may she follow after you, if you broke hers, may she forgive you, and may both of you find peace."

Joey shivered. "Thanks." She'd toyed, briefly, with the idea of hitting on Goblin, just to have the distraction, to cure the pain that threatened to swamp her whenever she thought about it. Now it was the furthest thought from her mind. All that adventuring had gotten her into this fix, where nobody wanted her. No need to compound that. So Joey accepted Goblin in the role of a chance bar companion, a neighbor, and settled down. She ordered her second whisky and took her tie off.

Goblin sipped at her ginger ale.

"Let me ask you something. Your friend, the king of the dykes?"

"Yes?"

"She have any role models when she was young?"

Goblin chortled. "My pop was one of hers. Rhea was another."

"Rhea?"

"My stepmom."

"So your parents were the exemplars of the queer community?"

"Yeah, I guess you could put it that way."

"Damn. I would have traded my soul to grow up knowing queer adults. To even see them, from a distance, know they exist," Joey said.

"Where you from?"

"Eden."

"We have to get ourselves back to the garden," Goblin said, and laughed. Joey felt around for her anger, couldn't find it, and laughed with her.

"That is kind of funny."

"Did you find Adam and Steve in the garden?"

"Just Steve, my best friend and a blazing light of gayitude. We broke out together."

"That is really great, and deserves a toast." Goblin motioned to the barpoet. "Kristie, another round, my good woman."

"You gotta be careful with the hard stuff," Joey said, looking at the ginger ale in the pint glass.

"This? This is nothing. The hard stuff is what is making you drink."

Joey took up her glass again at the suggestion. "Sad, but true. How do you feel about love?"

"I'm a big fan," Goblin said.

"I'm an addict. I get so stupid when I'm near it that I cannot be trusted. I don't think I can ever do that again."

"So what, you're swearing off the stuff for life?" Goblin asked.

"Something like that."

"That's the most ridiculous thing I've ever heard."

"Pardon?"

"Ridiculous. You are looking at love as a luxury, or an ornament. It's more like food. If you have an eating disorder, you don't stop eating. You learn how to do it in healthy ways, and relate well to your body."

"Huh."

"Sorry, I get a little high-handed sometimes. I get that from my stepmom."

"No, I appreciate it. I hadn't thought about it like that."

"You want another?" Goblin said.

Joey took a moment to think about it. "No, thanks. I think I'm good. I'm going to head home. Thanks for the company, neighbor."

"See you around." Goblin said, shaking her hand.

Chapter Fifteen

Joey got to the street and stood, undecided. Steve's apartment to her left. Leela's to the right. She stood, listening, thinking.

The yelp was high, clear, and pained, startling Joey out of her reverie. Too close at hand, in the small grassy alley between the Jamaican food shop and the closed antiques shop, three teenage boys crouched over a supine, squirming dog. The whining was heart rending. Joey was moving before she knew it, shouting, gesturing. If she had stopped to think about it, she might have thought better of it, but the surprise and momentum took the trio's attention away from the dog, a medium-sized mutt who snapped his body nearly in half trying to get away from the boot on his throat. Two of the boys wore hooded sweatshirts, one had a baseball cap on, skewed to the side. All held cigarettes that they had been putting out on the dog's flank. Smoke still curled from his fur. After placing the interruption, they stood their ground, not releasing the dog.

The ignorant cruelty of it enraged her. They were torturing a weaker creature for amusement, a creature that couldn't possibly understand and only wanted to please them. The dog had no choice whose hands it ended up in. The obscenity of the misuse of power, highlighted by the dog's high-pitched howling, decided it. She was among them the next moment, flailing, hands set against the chest of one with his boot on the dog's neck. He was easiest to shove back and away, his boot lifted, and the dog responded by skittering away violently toward the street. Joey glanced after him, glad to see him free, and took her eyes off the other two. It was a mistake a trained fighter wouldn't have made. It cost her three blows, one to the side of her head, cigarette still in hand, one to her shoulder, ripping the suit coat diagonally, and one more to the back of her leg, aimed at taking her down. It didn't work.

Once the surprise of being struck passed, the pain was negligible, particularly with the adrenaline that sung and howled in her veins. Joey held up her hands and faced them. Pride suffused Joey, buoying her up. She might well get beaten to a pulp, but the dog was free. That was what mattered. Power could be used to protect, preserve as well. Joey laughed.

It was the laugh that did it. This now bloodied woman, in a torn suit, was weaving above the space the dog used to be, hands held up like a clumsy boxer, laughing with delight. They didn't know what to make of it, and Joey could see it, from their milling hesitation to attack.

"Go ahead, motherfucker. Try me." It wasn't exactly gladiator-worthy dialogue, Joey thought, but it worked. It didn't matter now, how the fight ended. She'd seen something wrong and moved to make it right. One by one, they backed away, one sneaker at a time, toward the street. One broke and ran, the other two followed. It was over almost before it began.

Joey was left shaking her head to clear it. She shrugged out of her suit coat and examined the rip. It was beyond saving. *My only suit*, Joey thought. The side of her head was wet. Her thigh ached abominably, right above the knee, steadily, now that the adrenaline was fading. Nerves twitching, she walked to the street and looked around for the dog, but he was long gone. Joey was left standing in the circle before Nietzsche's.

There was a difference, Joey thought, between giving power to someone you trust, knowing that they will treat that gift with respect, and having it taken from you. Naomi had always wielded hers with respect. Psycho Barbie, never. Joey knew that she could say no at any point and have autonomy again. The strange alchemy of power, in relationships, distilled. There had to be an exchange of trust, or the power was useless. *Trust in the partner*, Joey thought, *and trust in yourself. There is no substitute for what I have learned*, Joey thought, *and no way to learn it except by trial.*

Funny how all the power of the threats only worked if I collaborated, Joey thought. *They stopped having power when I stopped giving it to them. Power isn't a new conversation, but it is never easy. Not your own power. You can hear the cliché every ten minutes and not have it make any difference. Until, one morning, you just get tired of maintaining the bullshit. It's not a stand up and shake your fist in the face of God kind of revolution, it's more like you need some rest and can't get it, so you sit down.*

Naomi had treated her like a king. Their time was exquisite all the more for the shared understanding that it was a perfect moment, and then gone. Ephemeral. It had shown Joey how to understand and appreciate the artfulness of that, of crafting a scene. Joey thought she didn't have much to offer Naomi when they started, but that time with her gave Joey back a sense of herself as a lover.

There are things that you do not allow yourself to think, unless someone gives you permission. Naomi had given her permission to think about, and explore, power, relationship, self-respect. Without that, Joey knew, she'd never be ready for the next great leap. The idea formed in Joey's head, whole and complete, like a fog burning away from a lake under the morning sun.

We never learn the things we need before we need to practice them. You don't learn how to leave someone you once loved, how to recognize duty and responsibility as belonging to yourself, as well as to another. To know that there is a way to do everything well, even leave. To divorce well. To bear yourself with dignity, to keep what you believe to be right, and do what you think best with all the grace that you can.

To accept endings as a portion of beginnings, and balance sadness with that knowledge. Everything ends. Everything begins. There are no clean lines to either. Sometimes the right thing will only seem so in looking back. That our thoughts are as colored by our environment as our emotions. That both can grow and change. Sometimes doing the right thing is doing the right thing for yourself and will only look like the right thing to you. That for all your love for them, you cannot lead someone else's life for them. You cannot let them lead your life for you. You can try. It isn't about morality, or goodness, or blame—merely a matter of what works.

Trying to give up everything about yourself to please another simply doesn't work. You may set it aside, for a time. But you will come back, haunting, in small ways, until you start to dream again in your own language. You can try to be someone else, but you will start to recognize yourself under that person's skin. That being happy isn't a side effect, or inconsequential. It is the goal, the endpoint, and every moment along the way. Nothing else. Life is fire and passion, friendship and love and never has to be less. You can experience profound, subtle, complex joy every single day; you can be struck by the love you have for the people around you, your city, your home, your work, your art, every time you meet them. Every time. It doesn't have to be dust and ashes, eaten like bread. Life has blood and juice to it, and is meant to. *We are meant for joy. I was never told that, but I learned it*, Joey thought. *It almost cost me everything I had, including breathing. But only almost.*

She turned right and headed for Leela's.

❖

Joey rang the bell. It had been too long since she'd seen Leela. Now, in the aftermath of the fight, all she wanted was to talk to her. Leela was the person she wanted to tell. Silence answered the bell. Was it too late? Maybe Leela hadn't come back here after she left the church.

Then the footsteps, down the stairs, and the creak of the door, opening.

"Hi," Joey said, unable to say much else. Leela was there, in a sweatshirt, hair mussed, eyes shadowed, looking haunted and tired. She brushed at her cheeks impatiently. "Don't you dare say hello to me now. You wouldn't say hello to me when you saw me at the church."

"Um, sorry."

"Sorry for saying hello or for not saying hello?" Leela demanded.

"Both. I owe you a raft of apologies. Can I come in?"

"What, now you want to talk? Did your date go home?"

"No, I left."

Leela stepped out on the porch, and saw the state Joey was in. Her mien changed abruptly. "What happened to you?" Her hands went to the side of Joey's head.

"Got into a fight in the alley next the antique shop. Couple boys were putting out cigarettes on a dog."

"God. You're a mess. You're bleeding."

"There were three of them," Joey said proudly. "The dog got away."

"Come upstairs. I want to clean that cut, at least."

Joey followed Leela up and sat down on the couch. She set the ruined jacket down next to her. Leela went to the kitchen and came back with a wet cloth. She sat down and gingerly dabbed at Joey's temple.

"Ashes?"

"He was holding a cigarette when he hit me."

Joey heard Leela make a sound in her throat, a cross between worry and condemnation. She set the towel aside and applied a bandage. "The cut is shallow and I cleaned it out. How does your head feel?"

Joey shrugged. "Not so bad, compared to my leg. Shoulder is a little sore. The coat's a total loss."

Leela opened her mouth, then turned away. "Well, you're a fool to go rushing down three boys on your own."

"Had to. I was the one that was there. Come on, you would have, too."

"Of course I would have. I just wouldn't have gotten hit," Leela said tartly. "What about your date? She not an animal lover?" Leela's voice had the bite of anger back in it.

"She wasn't, it wasn't, a date. It was a farewell."

Leela got up and walked back to the kitchen and rinsed her hands. "Oh, you break up with her, too?"

"We weren't dating. We were spending time, and it was time to end it."

"Why?" Leela's back was to Joey. Her hands gripped the granite countertop.

Joey walked up behind her softly, but Leela knew she was there.

"Leela—"

"None of that. You don't get to say my name."

"Okay."

"Stop agreeing with me."

"If you insist."

Leela turned around. "You don't get to do this. You don't get to waltz in here and rip my heart to pieces with your stupid head wound and saving puppies and—"

"I know."

"I get to say my piece, then you can go back to your wild and crazy life of heartbreaking. I'm about to be bakka crazy emotional, and you are just not ready for that."

"Leela, I'm not going to go."

"Fine. Let's test that, shall we? I'll make it worthwhile. It's time someone said it to you. You're being stupid. This whole my heart is an impenetrable fortress crap? Maudlin self-pitying nonsense. Steve knows it and won't say it to you." Leela muscled on ahead. "He loves you too much and thinks you'll snap out of it. But it's not like that. Love's a football game, and you are on the sidelines. You gotta suit up and play. It doesn't matter at all that you were dumb as a box of rocks about girls in the past. Everybody is. You're part of the audience, or you're in the play, and, Joey, you are not audience. You are totally awesome and it makes me crazy. Stop holding yourself back."

"You're right," Joey said simply.

"I'm what?" Leela stepped back.

"You're right. About all of it. It is self-pitying, and I'm good and tired of it. My heart's a block of Swiss cheese. Who am I kidding? I'm soft as butter."

"Soft is good," Leela said, stepping back in. "It makes you run down alleys to save puppies."

"Makes me react like I'm the only person who ever had a bad relationship. I'm sorry about that, Leela. I'm working on it, and I promise, I will keep that Swiss cheese in a safe location."

"I'll take good care of it. Let me, baby." Leela nudged at Joey. "Let me, dude."

Joey let go of the cliff she'd been clinging to, dropped right into laughter, and was free. "Did you seriously just call me dude?"

"God, we're sappy bastards," Leela said.

"We're going to be one of those couples that make people sick," Joey said.

"So we're a couple now?"

"If you want," Joey said, and shrugged. "Ouch." Leela hit her on the injured shoulder.

"Don't play. So, we are really a couple now? It's okay for me to say certain things to you?"

"Yeah. It is."

"You won't freak out on me and bolt?"

"No."

"I'm in love with you." Leela waited, watching Joey carefully. When Joey smiled, slowly, and didn't run, she continued as if she hadn't been understood. "Like big emotion love you."

"I love you, too."

"Shut up."

"No, really."

Leela kissed Joey, gingerly. "I guess we better do something about that, then."

She took Joey's hand.

"You know, we haven't lit a fire in the bedroom yet."

About the Author

Susan Smith was a founding member of the HAG Theatre Company in Buffalo, New York. After a decade of performing and writing for the stage, Smitty turned back to her first love, writing novels. Like most of the artists in hardworking Buffalo, Smitty keeps a full-time day job as a librarian and college instructor, while occasionally being enticed by drag shows and theatre projects. Along with her partner, the drag king Johnny Class, Smitty divides her time between Toronto and Buffalo. Traveling is good for the soul and borders are made to be crossed.

Books Available From Bold Strokes Books

A Guarded Heart by Jennifer Fulton. The last place FBI Special Agent Pat Roussel expects to find herself is assigned to an illicit private security gig baby-sitting a celebrity. (Ebook) (978-1-60282-067-8)

Saving Grace by Jennifer Fulton. Champion swimmer Dawn Beaumont, injured in a car crash she caused, flees to Moon Island, where scientist Grace Ramsay welcomes her. (Ebook) (978-1-60282-066-1)

The Sacred Shore by Jennifer Fulton. Successful tech industry survivor Merris Randall does not believe in love at first sight until she meets Olivia Pearce. (Ebook) (978-1-60282-065-4)

Passion Bay by Jennifer Fulton. Two women from different ends of the earth meet in paradise. Author's expanded edition. (Ebook) (978-1-60282-064-7)

Never Wake by Gabrielle Goldsby. After a brutal attack, Emma Webster becomes a self-sentenced prisoner inside her condo—until the world outside her window goes silent. (Ebook) (978-1-60282-063-0)

The Caretaker's Daughter by Gabrielle Goldsby. Against the backdrop of a nineteenth-century English country estate, two women struggle to find love. (Ebook) (978-1-60282-062-3)

Simple Justice by John Morgan Wilson. When a pretty-boy cokehead is murdered, former LA reporter Benjamin Justice and his reluctant new partner, Alexandra Templeton, must unveil the real killer. (978-1-60282-057-9)

Remember Tomorrow by Gabrielle Goldsby. Cees Bannigan and Arieanna Simon find that a successful relationship rests in remembering the mistakes of the past. (978-1-60282-026-5)

Put Away Wet by Susan Smith. Jocelyn "Joey" Fellows has just been savagely dumped—when she posts an online personal ad, she discovers more than just the great sex she expected. (978-1-60282-025-8)

Homecoming by Nell Stark. Sarah Storm loses everything that matters—family, future dreams, and love—will her new "straight" roommate cause Sarah to take a chance at happiness? (978-1-60282-024-1)

The Three by Meghan O'Brien. A daring, provocative exploration of love and sexuality. Two lovers, Elin and Kael, struggle to survive in a postapocalyptic world. (Ebook) (978-1-60282-056-2)

Falling Star by Gill McKnight. Solley Rayner hopes a few weeks with her family will help heal her shattered dreams, but she hasn't counted on meeting a woman who stirs her heart. (978-1-60282-023-4)

Lethal Affairs by Kim Baldwin and Xenia Alexiou. Elite operative Domino is no stranger to peril, but her investigation of journalist Hayley Ward will test more than her skills. (978-1-60282-022-7)

A Place to Rest by Erin Dutton. Sawyer Drake doesn't know what she wants from life until she meets Jori Diamantina—only trouble is, Jori doesn't seem to share her desire. (978-1-60282-021-0)

Warrior's Valor by Gun Brooke. Dwyn Izsontro and Emeron D'Artansis must put aside personal animosity and unwelcome attraction to defeat an enemy of the Protector of the Realm. (978-1-60282-020-3)

Finding Home by Georgia Beers. Take two polar-opposite women with an attraction for one another they're trying desperately to ignore, throw in a far-too-observant dog, and then sit back and enjoy the romance. (978-1-60282-019-7)

Word of Honor by Radclyffe. All Secret Service Agent Cameron Roberts and First Daughter Blair Powell want is a small intimate wedding, but the paparazzi and a domestic terrorist have other plans. (978-1-60282-018-0)

Hotel Liaison by JLee Meyer. Two women searching through a secret past discover that their brief hotel liaison is only the beginning. Will they risk their careers—and their hearts—to follow through on their desires? (978-1-60282-017-3)

Love on Location by Lisa Girolami. Hollywood film producer Kate Nyland and artist Dawn Brock discover that love doesn't always follow the script. (978-1-60282-016-6)

Edge of Darkness by Jove Belle. Investigator Diana Collins charges at life with an irreverent comment and a right hook, but even those may not protect her heart from a charming villain. (978-1-60282-015-9)

Thirteen Hours by Meghan O'Brien. Workaholic Dana Watts's life takes a sudden turn when an unexpected interruption arrives in the form of the most beautiful breasts she has ever seen—stripper Laurel Stanley's. (978-1-60282-014-2)

In Deep Waters 2 by Radclyffe and Karin Kallmaker. All bets are off when two award-winning authors deal the cards of love and passion... and every hand is a winner. (978-1-60282-013-5)

Pink by Jennifer Harris. An irrepressible heroine frolics, frets, and navigates through the "what ifs" of her life: all the unexpected turns of fortune, fame, and karma. (978-1-60282-043-2)

Deal with the Devil by Ali Vali. New Orleans crime boss Cain Casey brings her fury down on the men who threatened her family, and blood and bullets fly. (978-1-60282-012-8)

Naked Heart by Jennifer Fulton. When a sexy ex-CIA agent sets out to seduce and entrap a powerful CEO, there's more to this plan than meets the eye...or the flogger. (978-1-60282-011-1)

Heart of the Matter by KI Thompson. TV newscaster Kate Foster is Professor Ellen Webster's dream girl, but Kate doesn't know Ellen exists...until an accident changes everything. (978-1-60282-010-4)

Heartland by Julie Cannon. When political strategist Rachel Stanton and dude ranch owner Shivley McCoy collide on an empty country road, fate intervenes. (978-1-60282-009-8)

Shadow of the Knife by Jane Fletcher. Militia Rookie Ellen Mittal has no idea just how complex and dangerous her life is about to become. A Celaeno series adventure romance. (978-1-60282-008-1)

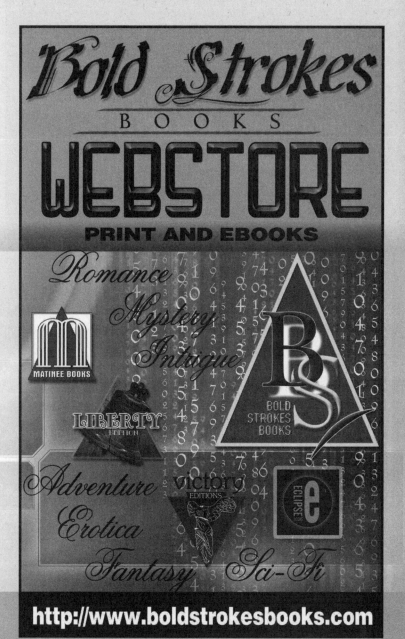